ELLIOT SKELL

Neversuch House

Night of the
Black Condor

SIMON AND SCHUSTER

First published in Great Britain in 2011 by Simon and Schuster UK Ltd,
A CBS COMPANY

Simon & Schuster UK Ltd
1st Floor, 222 Gray's Inn Road, London WC1X 8HB

Text copyright © Elliot Skell 2011

A CIP catalogue record for this book is available from the British Library.

ISBN 978-1-84738-43-1

1 3 5 7 9 10 8 6 4 2

Printed in the UK by Cox & Wyman, Reading RG1 8EX.

www.simonandschuster.co.uk

In memory of
Evelina Hartslip Codd
whose early death remains a mystery

1

In the Hall of Puppets

The wheels on the chair squeaked. It was an old chair made of wicker, and the wheels were of rubber that had hardened and cracked with age. They squeaked as the chair moved up the room, were silent as it stopped, and then squeaked as it moved again.

It was more of a hall than a room, long, high-ceilinged, with a row of glass lanterns that hung from the roof and gave off a yellow light. The floor was marble and the walls on both sides were lined with shelves of red wood, right to the top.

Gazing down from the shelves, all the way along the Hall in row upon row, right up to the ceiling, were faces.

They were made of wood, of papier mâché, of porcelain, of wax. Some were small, some were big. Some laughed, some sneered. Some had bodies with strings attached, others a simple tube of cloth through which a hand could be inserted. There were faces of innocent children and faces of witches with crimson skin and flaming eyes, faces of gentle giants and faces of howling, screeching imps. In the yellow of the lantern light, it was as if the whole world was represented there, in all its goodness and evil.

But the only real person in the room was the man in the wheelchair. He was old, and wore a blue coat with gold braid that looked as if it was modelled on an ancient sea captain's costume. The strands of white hair on his head were few, but they were long, and came down to the collar of his coat. He had a flattened nose and his lips were pressed together in a kind of permanent snarl. His chin was sunk on his chest, and because of the stiffness of his neck, he couldn't raise his head. The only way he could look at the shelves was by straining his eyes up in their sockets.

On his right hand he wore an enormous ruby ring. The ring glinted and flashed as he turned the wheels with his hands.

He pushed himself along the Hall, stopping here and there to roll his eyes up and stare at one of the figures, then moving on. The squeaking of the wheels, which sometimes reached an almost ear-splitting note, didn't annoy him. It annoyed others and helped keep them away.

He stopped again. His eyes rested on a figure on one of the shelves. It had a cunning, spiteful face with a sharp nose and piercing black eyes. The old man stared at it, a memory going through his mind.

He heard a noise behind him. He couldn't turn his head enough to see where it came from. He heard footsteps.

'Who is it?' he demanded, frowning, listening for an answer. 'Who's there?'

There was no reply.

He pushed one of the wheels, holding the other still. The chair turned with a terrible screech.

Behind him stood a young man dressed in black, a cloak over his shoulders with a long hood that hung down his back.

'What do you want?' demanded the old man.

'I've been told to come and get you.'

'You? You've never been sent for me before. Where are Wilson and Tate?'

'They've been called away.'

'Called away? Called away to do what? What could be more important than coming to get me?'

The young man shrugged.

'You're by yourself. It needs two men to carry me down.'

'I'll manage.'

The old man sniffed. 'You're too early. Didn't they tell you what time to come? Go away and come back with someone else.'

'I've been told to come now.'

'It's too early!' said the old man angrily. 'All I ask for is one hour alone here each week. That's all I've ever asked for since I was forced to wear this coat. Is that too much? Can't I even have that?'

'It's not my decision. I do as I'm told.'

'Then do as you're told and go away and come back with someone else in half an hour!'

The young man shook his head. He walked across to the chair, took hold of the handles at the back and began to push.

The old man tried to grab the wheels, but he was too frail to resist the younger man's strength and the wheels slipped through his grip. Their screeching drowned out his voice as he shouted.

They reached the doorway at the end of the Hall. A long, straight staircase ran down for over a hundred steps. The Hall itself was at the top of a building that towered above a covered courtyard. Even after he had begun using a wheelchair, the old man had refused to have his puppets moved to a place which would have been easier to get to. Each week he had to be carried up the staircase and carried back down to the bottom, where another wicker wheelchair awaited him.

The staircase was in front of him. The steep stone steps ran down as far as he could see.

'I'm telling you,' he snapped, 'you'll need two men to take me down!'

'Not today,' said the man behind him, and he gave the wheelchair a push.

2

Back

This is the story of Omnia Halibut and the extraordinary events that befell her at the age of twelve and a quarter. Omnia wasn't present in the Hall of Puppets when the crime that I have described took place. In fact, she had never been up the long flight of stairs that lead to the Hall, although she had heard of it. And yet what happened there would soon involve her in a story so extraordinary that there may be some readers – not many, I hope – who might even doubt that it is true.

But before we begin, you need to understand how a place such as the Hall of Puppets came to exist, and why an old man in a blue sea captain's coat with a huge ruby ring on his hand came to be sitting there in a wheelchair. In other words, as often happens, before we go forward, we need to go back.

Back to a time long before Omnia was born, a hundred

years back, and then another hundred years back, and then even further back until we arrive at a misty night under a moonless sky when a boat landed at a deserted beach near the small town of Pettifog and out stepped Captain Everdew C Halibut. He brought with him six large chests, tightly sealed, and a small man called Digby. After they unloaded the chests, Captain Halibut and Digby burned the boat on the beach, creating a flame that was just visible to the harbour master at the top of the Pettifog lighthouse. No one would ever discover how Captain Halibut and Digby spent that night, nor what became of the chests. At dawn, the two men headed into the wilderness. When the harbour master arrived the next morning to investigate, he found only the blackened embers of their boat, already floating away on the tide.

For three years, nothing was seen of the Captain or his helper. Later, rumours spread about what they did in that time. Some claimed they had been spotted digging for diamonds in the deep gullies of the mountain ranges. Others claimed to have been held up and robbed on remote, lonely roads by two men answering their description. Others claimed to have spoken to people who knew people who had seen them on a vast plantation in a valley far to the west – or sometimes it was far to the south, or far to the north – where thousands of workers laboured for them like slaves. Still others would later claim that the huge fortune of Everdew C Halibut arrived with him, in fact, on that very first night, in the six sealed chests, and had been lying buried on the beach outside Pettifog all the time while the Captain and his helper were away.

Whatever the truth, three years after that night, the two men emerged from the wilderness and marched into the town. The Captain took a room at the grandest hotel and let it be known that he wanted to buy land. Word spread that he was paying in gold and wouldn't quibble over the price. Soon a queue snaked along the street and into the hotel and up the stairs and down the corridor to the Captain's room, where he sat behind a table facing the door, ready to dole out his money. No one who glimpsed him that day would ever forget the sight. He wore a blue sea captain's coat with gold braid and a huge ruby ring glinted on his finger.

The mayor came first, waving deeds for useless land outside the town that nobody wanted. The Captain snapped them up. He took any other piece of land he could buy in the vicinity. By the end of the day, he had acquired a vast estate of hills and valleys, lakes and streams, dense woods and swampy marsh, ten times the size of the town itself.

And where was the Captain's helper while the Captain was buying his estate? The small, strange man was scouring the streets of Pettifog, whispering into the ear of anyone who looked strong enough to lift a brick or use a shovel. Shop assistants came out from behind their counters, drunks looked up in amazement and rose from the gutter. Soon there was barely an able-bodied worker left to help with the running of Pettifog. Owners of the town's businesses came into the streets and gazed at each other in dismay. The next morning, Captain Halibut and Digby marched out of the town with all the people they had employed, and the shopkeepers, seeing their customers and assistants marching away, had little choice but to lock their shops and join the procession.

Pettifog was deserted. The mist that blew in from the sea filled the streets and settled over an empty town. Visitors arrived to find boarded-up windows and padlocked doors. But very few of them cared, because almost all of them were on their way to the Captain's estate themselves.

The Captain and his helper sent for skilled workmen, and for every one they summoned, another ten, or fifty, or a hundred answered the call. On the Captain's new estate there was work for all. Masons, carpenters, carvers, bricklayers, tilers, plumbers, plasterers, painters and labourers of every description and nationality passed through the empty streets of Pettifog, all drawn by rumours of the great construction taking place north of the town. An army of workers has to be cared for, and doctors, dentists, cooks and tailors soon followed in their wake. On the Captain's new estate outside Pettifog, an enormous camp had developed, dedicated entirely to the Captain's work.

First, a wall appeared, running for miles all the way around the edge of the vast expanse of land that the Captain had purchased. Then a building began to rise on one of the hills deep inside the estate, and continued rising until it had become a soaring tower with a pair of huge round windows at the top. Other structures rose around it. Buildings spread over the land like the crust of a thick fungus growing from its spore. A forest of turrets and spires and chimneys sprouted from their roofs. The plans for the seemingly never-ending construction came out of one of the six sealed chests, and the Captain sat for hours perusing them or walking from place to place with the plans rolled up under his arm and Digby by his side to shout instructions and check the progress of the work. No one saw the plans but the Captain and his helper, and so vast was the building that only they knew every part that was being built. No one else could say exactly how big it was or how each part connected with the others.

Later, there would be a rumour that the Captain and Digby secretly constructed a room for the Captain's treasure at the heart of the building, beneath the Great Tower itself, excavating down to the very bedrock. Another version of the rumour said that the secret room was built by a dozen specially selected men. But no one could ever find a man who had been one of this dozen, and whether they disappeared after the room was built – perhaps killed and buried under the very floor they had laid – or whether they never existed in the first place, no one would ever know.

The work went on for five back-breaking years, and after five years, a monstrous cluster of buildings and towers stood in the middle of the estate, surrounded by fields and woods and marsh, like an island of soaring cliffs and pinnacles within a landlocked sea. So vast was the estate that it was a distance of miles from the buildings at its heart to the wall around it. In this wall, the Captain had allowed only a single gate. With the work finished, the army of workers was driven out and the gate locked behind them.

As they left, they looked back and saw that two words had been carved in the stone over the gate. Those who could read spoke the words to those who couldn't. The name spread like a hissing whisper.

Neversuch House.

So the House was completed, although it was a house only in name, and not even as a mansion or a palace would the description be sufficient for the gigantic, grotesque thing that had risen outside the town of Pettifog. In this gigantic thing, as far as anyone knew, behind the wall that encircled it, in its echoing corridors and on its dizzying staircases, in its thousands of rooms and attics and turrets, only the Captain and his helper lived.

The Captain had named his construction Neversuch House because never such a house had been constructed – or even thought of before – as the one that now stood inside the long wall with its single gate. But the people of Pettifog soon wished that never such a house had been built. After the work was finished, they went back to their homes and unlocked their doors and unboarded their windows, but life in the town wasn't the same as before.

The townspeople felt that they were always under

observation. There was no place that was out of sight of the dark, soaring tower at the centre of the House. The pair of windows at the very summit watched like a pair of wide-open, never-blinking eyes. People imagined that the two inhabitants of the House, the Captain and his helper, were each standing in one of them, looking down. When their children misbehaved, they said the Captain would see and come down to take them away. They wished they had never helped to build the House. Only now, when it was too late, did they understand what they had done. They had taken the Captain's money to build a place that would stand over them forever.

But the Captain, even if he was watching from the tower, didn't come down to take their naughty children. He was never seen outside the walls of the estate, not after the day he drove the last of the workers out and closed the gate behind them.

Yet gradually, the House did acquire other inhabitants. Digby appeared from time to time in the town, and on each occasion, a day or two later, one of the townspeople took the road to the House, and waited before the gate, and entered as servant or gardener or carpenter or cook, never to be seen again. People said that if the Captain's helper approached you, he would offer as much money as it took until you agreed to go to the House. Some lived in fear of his approach, others lived in hope. And ships began arriving in Pettifog loaded with goods for the House, which was utterly bare when the workers departed. Furniture, carpets, tapestries, paintings, silver and every other kind of luxury – or so the townspeople imagined – arrived in crates at the docks. The innumerable rooms of the House seemed to have an insatiable appetite for furnishings, all of the finest. The wagon-drivers of Pettifog unloaded the goods in front of the gate and drove away, and some time later, the goods disappeared into the House and no one ever saw who came out to get them.

One day, about ten years after the House was built, a ship arrived at Pettifog with a different type of cargo. When the ship docked, a beautiful young woman and two maids disembarked. The Captain's helper was waiting for them in a covered carriage. He took the woman and her two maids away and the gate of Neversuch House closed behind them. A couple of days later, the mayor of the town was summoned to the House. Sworn to secrecy, and paid handsomely for his silence, he never revealed what he had seen or done there. But the following day, a certificate was deposited in the town office, recording the marriage of Mademoiselle Begonia Frieslander and Captain Everdew C Halibut.

Over the next fourteen years, six birth certificates were deposited at the town office. A year after the marriage, a son arrived who was named Evergreen H Halibut. A second son followed, Evertrue V Halibut. Then came three daughters, Ribonia Halibut, Estonia Halibut and Yvonnia Halibut. Finally, five years after Yvonnia, a last son, Everwell X Halibut, came into the world.

Twelve years after the arrival of the sixth and last child,

and forty-three years to the day after he came ashore with his six sealed chests, the death certificate of the old Captain, Everdew C Halibut, was deposited in its turn.

So the pattern was set. Over the next two hundred years, the Halibuts and the town would flourish side by side – the Halibuts behind the wall of Neversuch House, the town outside it – neither one knowing nor caring much about the other.

Behind the wall, one generation of Halibuts gave rise to the next, still living on the vast fortune of the old Captain. From time to time, someone would arrive in Pettifog and be driven to the House, and a few days later, a new marriage certificate would appear in the town office. Then there would be birth certificates, and eventually death certificates. Alongside the Halibuts lived whole families of servants, descendants of the servants that the Captain's helper, Digby, had lured to the gate, passing on their skills from one generation to the next as they served one generation of Halibut after another.

Outside the wall, the world changed. Wars were fought, nations formed, discoveries were made, inventions perfected. Populations grew, and Pettifog developed from a small town into a city, spreading west from the coast, and then south, and eventually it even spread north around the edge of the Halibut estate. But the House remained, closed off by the wall that the workers had built in the time of the old Captain, covering almost as much area as the entire city outside its gates.

If you had been able to observe it, year after year, decade after decade, you might have thought that nothing behind that wall ever altered, not even the servants. In Neversuch House, tradition was everything. And if you think that after two hundred years it must have been a strange kind of world in there, you would be right. Stranger than you can imagine, unless your imagination is very strange. But let me say one thing. Your own world, which is so familiar and understandable to you, might seem equally peculiar to someone coming from far away. Or to put it another way, no world is strange to those who have known nothing else.

But to return to the Halibuts . . . Within the House, the Halibuts never formally chose a leader. As in so many things, they developed their own peculiar way. In each generation there had always been a new leader favoured by the previous one. Nowhere was it written down that the favoured one must be the next Captain of the House, as the leader of the Halibuts was called, but nowhere was it written down that this one mustn't. So in every generation, the favoured one become the new Captain after the previous one had died. Sometimes it was a son, sometimes a nephew, sometimes a cousin, sometimes someone else altogether who was chosen to wear the ruby ring and a blue coat modelled after the coat that Everdew C Halibut himself had worn.

When the First Captain died, his son, Evertrue V Halibut, was the chosen candidate. Then followed Evertrue's nephew, called Everdew in memory of the First

Captain, then Evercalm, Evergreen, Everdew the Third, Evernew, Evertrue the Second, Everdew the Fourth and finally Everwise B Halibut, who led the House for twenty-four years.

By the time he turned eighty-seven, he was frail and quarrelsome, and thought only of the puppets that he had collected before becoming Captain. For three years he had been confined to his wicker wheelchairs, and for a further three years before that he had been unable to climb the stairs of the Great Tower, which a Captain of the Halibuts was expected to do each year on Landing Day, the anniversary of the First Captain's arrival. By the time he was sent tumbling down the stairs of the Hall of Puppets, Everwise was so old and frail that everyone thought his death couldn't be far away, although no one was expecting it to happen quite in the way that it did. Wilson and Tate, the two attendants who normally came to collect him after his weekly visit to the Hall, were delayed on their way for a few minutes – when they arrived, they found Everwise dead at the bottom of the stairs.

Eldred Sturgeon, the Chief Physician of the House and head of the Sturgeon family who had served as doctors since the days of the First Captain, announced after examining the body that Everwise had died from falling down the stairs, which just about anyone could have worked out for themselves. As to why he had fallen, Eldred Sturgeon had no idea and didn't see why he should be expected to, just because he was a doctor.

No one could find anything to suggest that a suspicious event had taken place. The Hall of Puppets looked as it always did, with no evidence that any kind of struggle or confrontation had occurred. It seemed clear that Everwise's death was an accident. Theories soon formed to explain how it had happened. So impatient had Everwise become in his old age, and so irritable, that when Wilson and Tate were late, he had probably decided to try to crawl down to his second wheelchair at the bottom of the stairs by himself, and had fallen while getting out of the chair at the top, taking the whole thing with him. Or else he had wheeled himself to the top of the stairs to call out to see if Wilson and Tate had arrived, and had mistakenly rolled himself over the edge. Or his hands had slipped on the wheels while wheeling himself backwards – as he sometimes did out of sheer contrariness – and he had pushed himself further than he meant to.

Some of the Halibuts described Everwise's death as an unfortunate accident, some as a remarkable accident, some even called it a freakish accident, but everyone agreed that an accident it was, caused by Everwise's own impatience and irritability.

So the truth of the crime was concealed and as far as the House was concerned, there was only one thing about the death that was worrying – Everwise had perished without revealing who he favoured to succeed him as Captain of the House. Not once in the twenty-four years of his Captainship – not by a word, a look, a wink – had he given a clue. As far as anyone was aware, this had never happened before. And in a world ruled entirely by the traditions of generations, no one knew quite what to do about it.

Yet he was dead and must be buried, that much was clear. And the burial must be performed among the grassy mounds in the place known as the Field of Dreams, as had the burial of every Captain of the House, and the new Captain must give the funeral speech for the one who had just died. But since Everwise had refused to reveal his choice of Captain before tumbling down the stairs with his wheelchair, no one knew who that should be.

Much discussion and debate took place. Records were searched, histories of the House consulted, and still no answer was found. There were no volunteers for the job. In the end, it was decided that the oldest Halibut living, and who was still capable of standing, would read the speech. This turned out to be a ninety-two-year-old man called Everdean P Halibut, who reacted with terror when he realised it was him.

Everdean was the unofficial geologist of the House and had never interested himself in anything but the rocks of the estate, of which he had built up a vast collection when he was younger. He wanted nothing but to continue studying them in peace with the equally vast collection of magnifying glasses and microscopes that he had accumulated. But he was too old and frail to resist as he was put into the ancient blue coat of the First Captain, had the ruby ring rammed on to his finger, and was dragged to the Field of Dreams.

So two days after the Captain's body was found at the bottom of the stairs to the Hall of Puppets, Everdean stood to deliver the funeral speech, and the burial of Everwise B Halibut, Tenth Captain of the House, took place.

Omnia Halibut was aged twelve years and a quarter on the day of Everwise's funeral. Twelve years and a quarter and three days to be precise, but we needn't quibble over the detail. There are more important things awaiting our attention. Omnia doesn't realise it yet – nor is there any reason that she should – but a series of extraordinary events is about to unfold, and she is going to be at the centre of them.

3

The Funeral in the Field of Dreams

It was no ordinary coffin. Made from black wood, it was huge, comfortably big enough for two people, with the crouched figure of an imp carved at each corner, teeth bared and hands clawed, as if waiting to spring at anyone who would dare to open the lid. It rested next to an open grave that had been dug in the Field of Dreams among the mounds that marked the places of previous burials.

On one side of the grave sat Everwise's widow, Allevia Halibut, on the red Mourner's Throne, which had a pair of the crouching imps carved on each of its armrests. The feet of the head mourner weren't supposed to touch the ground on the day of the funeral so the throne had been carried to the side of the grave with Allevia seated upon it. Behind her stood a throng of Halibuts. On the other side of the grave stood a throng of servants, led by a small, hunched man in a coat of green velvet, the hereditary Butler of the

House, great-great-great-great-great-great-grandson of the original Digby who had arrived with the First Captain.

Everdean, the reluctant reader of the funeral speech, stood at the head of the grave, flanked by two attendants who were there to support him if his legs gave way. He was perfectly bald and his smooth, egg-shaped head wobbled as he mumbled the words written on a paper in his shaky hand. The ancient coat of the First Captain, which was brought out only for the most solemn ceremonial occasions, was much too big for him. The cuffs came down almost to the ends of his fingers.

The funeral was taking time, even by the standards of a Halibut ceremony. The funeral speech for a Captain was supposed to be in rhyme, and at least thirty-eight verses long, and each verse had to have at least six lines – and as many as eight – and Everdean wasn't exactly the fastest reader in the world. Even the title was in rhyme. It was called *A Funeral Poem in Memory – Of a Most Desperacious Tragedy – The Death of a Captain Accidentally – On the Stairs to the Hall of Puppetry*, and it had taken Everdean about five minutes just to mumble his way through it.

Yet if you had been there, you might not have thought anything about the funeral was particularly unusual – apart from the impish gargoyles on the huge coffin, of course, and the lady on the red throne, and the way the spectators stood in two separate groups, and the fact that the man who was mumbling his way through the rhyming speech had turned up in an old, faded coat that obviously wasn't his – unless you happened to glance at the trees that stood around the Field of Dreams. Because if you had glanced in their direction, sooner or later you would have noticed a suspiciously large shape sitting in one of them. Too large to be a bird, or a squirrel, or anything else likely to be found in a tree. And once that had caught your attention, you would have noticed another, and another, and before long you would have realised they were all around the field, in every tree, sitting on branches, clinging to tree trunks, peering out through the leaves at the funeral taking place below them.

It was a tradition dating back to the time when Evergreen F Halibut was the Captain of the House that the Halibut children were allowed to watch funerals and certain other ceremonies from the trees. Evergreen, the Fifth Captain, had himself spent much of his time in the trees, particularly pine trees and cypresses, and although he couldn't get many of the adults to join him, he often held well-attended feasts for the children in tree houses he had the carpenters build across the estate. Nothing could be healthier for growing minds and growing limbs, in his opinion, than time spent in the branches.

That was over a hundred years ago, and the tree houses the carpenters built for Evergreen had fallen apart long before, torn to pieces by storms and rotted by rains. Yet the tradition of children in the trees lived on, as so many traditions did in Neversuch House, without any particular rhyme or reason. No one watched the children or told them how high they could climb. Occasionally one of them fell, plummeting out of a tree and hitting the ground with a thud during a funeral or some other ceremony, with obvious consequences.

You might think that allowing children to climb as high as they liked, entirely unsupervised and without any kind of safety equipment, showed carelessness on the part of the Halibut adults, or thoughtlessness, or even worse. But if a child climbed too high, or chose to sit on a branch too slender to carry its weight, or refused to take account of the wind on a blustery day, it was obviously either an idiot or a show-off and its loss was probably a blessing in disguise. Or so the Halibut adults would have said, if they had been asked. They had done exactly the same thing when they were children and they had all managed to grow up – those who hadn't plummeted out of a tree – and it hadn't hurt them.

Omnia herself was perched five branches up in a huge oak tree which was her favourite spot for funerals. On a branch that grew from the other side of the trunk at almost exactly the same level sat her cousin, Evergrow D Halibut. Evergrow was only a couple of months younger than Omnia, with brown hair cut in a straight line across his forehead, but he was small for his age. Some of the more malicious children called him Nevergrow.

'Can you hear anything?' Omnia said to him.

Evergrow shook his head.

Omnia listened harder, trying to make out the words

of the old man wafting up from the field below. He was mumbling so quietly that it must have been hard for the people around the grave to hear what he was saying, much less the children in the trees. Now and then, a word or two was carried on the breeze, too faint to be understood, like the bleating of a frightened lamb.

'This is ridiculous!' said Omnia.

'It can't be easy to make such a long speech,' said a girl sitting a couple of branches below them. Sororia Halibut was the kindest-hearted person Omnia knew, always trying to make up between the two sides when there was an argument and seeing the other person's point of view. Sometimes her kind-heartedness was so kind-hearted it was sickening.

Omnia glanced at Sororia doubtfully. The old man's voice hadn't been any louder when he started.

The faint bleating sound droned on. Omnia looked back at Everdean. Even the Halibut children knew that he couldn't seriously be the next Captain. As to how the new Captain would actually be chosen, that was still hopelessly beyond everyone, adult and child alike. A few people had suggested that Everwise might have left a clue in his will, which was to be read by the Butler at the feast following the funeral, and everyone was banking on that.

Omnia heard something whistling through the air. She looked up just in time to catch a pine cone that was flying at her head. In a tree not far away, a girl made a face at her.

Evesia Halibut was sitting next to her twin sister, Artesia, both wearing orange sunhats. The twins were almost identical in appearance and almost opposite in nature. Omnia was a great friend of Artesia, and for that reason, Evesia regarded her as a great enemy.

Evesia was especially hostile today and from time to time, as the funeral progressed, she was plucking pine cones out of the tree where she was sitting and hurling them at Omnia, trying to knock her off her branch. But after the first one brushed past her, Omnia was ready, listening for the sound of a cone whistling through the leaves, and if it came anywhere near her, she caught it. Then she would call out to Everblue J Halibut, a skinny boy of eight who was sitting in an elm tree not far to her left, and toss it to him, and Everblue would call out and toss it to someone else, and each of Evesia's pine cones went around the Field of Dreams from one tree to the next until someone dropped it.

Omnia didn't realise it, but this was exactly how traditions started in Neversuch House, and it was perfectly possible that in years to come, children would throw pine cones to each other whenever there was a funeral and no one would have any idea why they were doing it.

'Everblue,' Omnia called out, and she tossed the pine cone across to him.

Beside the grave, Everdean had been mumbling for over half an hour. The speech had been written by Pedagogia Halibut, Sororia's great-aunt on her mother's side. Pedagogia regarded herself as the chief poet of the

House and generally volunteered whenever a rhyme was needed. She also made a speciality of using as many long and complicated words as possible, which wasn't making things any easier for Everdean.

Another pine cone came whistling through the branches. Omnia caught it and grinned at Evesia before throwing it on to Everblue. Evesia scowled back at her from under her orange sunhat.

The bleating stopped. But the speech wasn't over. Everdean had merely paused to turn the paper over, which wasn't an easy matter, not only because of the trembling of his fingers but because the cuffs of the coat kept getting in the way. He might not have succeeded at all had not one of the attendants reached forward in exasperation and done it for him. On the Mourner's Throne, Allevia Halibut appeared to have fallen asleep.

Omnia glanced at her cousin and rolled her eyes. She had seen plenty of funerals and didn't think this one was particularly special. She had expected something extraordinary for a Captain's burial. After all, it had happened only nine times previously in the entire history of the House. Yet so far, it was turning out to be as boring as just about any other funeral.

'You have to admit,' she said to Evergrow, 'this is pretty disappointing.'

Evergrow nodded.

'You wouldn't be happy if you were the Captain of the House, and you were stuck in a wheelchair for all those years, and then you die in a freakish accident, and after all of that, this turned out to be the funeral you got.'

'Although you wouldn't be here to see it, I suppose,' said Evergrow.

'But if you *were*.'

'It's because we can't hear the speech,' said Sororia. 'Imagine if we could hear the speech! Imagine how special it would seem then.'

'Right, *really* special.' Omnia glanced at Evergrow and rolled her eyes again. Evergrow grinned. They had both heard plenty of Pedagogia's poems before and they weren't exactly the highlights of any occasion.

'I think you're being very harsh, Omnia,' said Sororia. 'Everdean's trying as hard as he can. It's not that bad.'

There's no answer to that, thought Omnia. Sororia believed anyone was being harsh unless they were being as kind-hearted as her – which was impossible, of course, because no one could be as kind-hearted as Sororia.

Omnia looked at Evergrow again. 'Are you hungry?'

Evergrow nodded.

'Let's just hope the feast makes up for this,' said Omnia, which was probably what everyone in the Field of Dreams was thinking as well.

Eventually, Everdean stopped again. This time he had finally finished the speech. Someone nudged Allevia and she jolted awake. Twelve of the servants came forward to lift the enormous coffin. Struggling to keep it level, they lowered it with ropes. It tilted sharply to one end and hit the bottom of the grave with a thud.

The servants stepped away, holding their backs. Everdean uttered the final words of the ceremony. Then there was silence. Everdean glanced at the Butler, checking if there was anything else he was meant to do. The Butler gave a slight shake of his head and gestured towards the other side of the field. Everdean gave a little start, then turned and began to shuffle across the Field of Dreams. Four servants raised the Mourner's Throne with Allevia on it and followed him. Then came the other Halibuts and then the rest of the servants, led by Digby. All around the field, children were dropping from the trees to join them.

At first, it was an orderly procession, winding its way between the grassy mounds. But Everdean led it so slowly that within a couple of minutes the procession had turned into a rout. The hungriest and the greediest walked fastest, hoping to get the best places at the feast. They swarmed around Everdean and Allevia and left them behind among the mounds.

The route to the feast led out of the Field of Dreams and up the stairs that ran behind the Bright Tower to a long terrace lined by columns. By the time Omnia reached the Tower, the stairs and the colonnade at the top were a heaving, chattering flood of Halibuts and servants. Omnia lost touch with Evergrow and Sororia, who were somewhere in the crowd around her. She reached the colonnade and the throng took her along in its stream towards the feast, where everyone was headed. Or not quite. Omnia glimpsed a dark figure slip between two columns and disappear.

She followed and came into a courtyard. On the other side the man was just about to open a door. He was wearing a black, hooded messenger's cloak.

'Wait!' cried Omnia.

The man turned. He was a tall, thin young man with deep-set eyes and sunken cheeks, and his name was Cornelius Slinker. He came from an ancient family of servants who had lived and worked at the House as messengers since the days of the First Captain. *Stealth, Silence, Speed*. That was the motto of the Slinkers, and Cornelius carried it further than most. He hardly ever spoke and always had a severe, watchful expression on his face. You only ever saw him slipping past, like a shadow on a wall, and usually he was gone by the time you realised you had seen him. None of the Halibut children liked Cornelius Slinker and quite a few were scared of him.

Omnia wasn't exactly scared of him, or at least not enough to outweigh her curiosity.

'Not going to the feast?' she said.

Cornelius shook his head.

Omnia came closer. 'Why not?'

'Got an errand,' said the messenger.

Omnia saw the corner of a big envelope protruding from the pocket of Slinker's black cloak. Cornelius noticed where she was looking and hurriedly pushed the envelope down.

'What's that?' said Omnia.

Cornelius didn't reply.

28

'Is that what you're taking? What is it?'

'Death certificate,' muttered the messenger.

'Everwise's?'

Cornelius nodded.

'And you're taking it to the city?'

The messenger nodded again.

'Can I have a look?'

Cornelius frowned.

Omnia came closer. 'It won't hurt anyone if I have a look, will it?' She put out her hand. 'Please.'

'Can't break the seal,' said Cornelius.

'Who'll know?'

He shook his head.

'Let me just see it.'

Cornelius put his hand over his pocket.

'Why not?'

Cornelius stared at her with his deep-set eyes. They didn't blink. They just gazed at her, unmoving.

His gaze was unnerving. Omnia had only followed him out of curiosity. She forced a laugh. 'You're going to miss the feast.'

'Butler told me to go.'

'And I suppose you always do as you're told?'

Cornelius nodded.

'But I just told you to show me the death certificate.'

The messenger's face didn't change. There was no hint of a smile. He opened the door, threw one last glance at Omnia, pulled his hood over his head, and disappeared.

Omnia could hear the noise of the crowd in the colonnade around the corner. She stood in the empty courtyard a moment longer. It was odd that Cornelius Slinker should miss the feast. Everyone was supposed to be there. But if the Butler had told him to go, he had to go. Yet why had the Butler told him? Why not wait until tomorrow?

And why wouldn't he even show her the envelope if it was only the Captain's death certificate?

At that moment, Omnia knew, the messenger would be making his way down to the West Range, a massive construction of corridors and apartments, and from there he would descend more stairs and cross more courtyards and go along more passages until he came to an arch far below the Range, which was one of the ways out of the huge cluster of the buildings of Neversuch House. From there he would trot for three miles, at a fast messenger's pace, until he reached the sole gate in the wall that ran around the estate.

And once the gate had been opened for him, Omnia knew, Cornelius Slinker would step out into the streets of the city that surrounded Neversuch House to deliver whatever it was that he was really carrying.

But Omnia could only imagine what that would be like. Like every other Halibut, she had never been out there.

4

The Feast in the Purple Nave

For twenty-four hours the fires in the ovens under the Great Kitchen Court had been blazing in preparation for the dead Captain's funeral feast. Now the food was piled high on tables that stood end to end along the length of the Purple Nave. There were huge trays of Everwise's favourite food, roasted pigeons stuffed with artichoke, in memory of the dead Captain, and every other type of roasted flesh as well. Thick yellow candles stood on the tables and others burned in tall holders along the walls. The Nave was a long hall with a high, vaulted ceiling. But it was damp, and since no work had been done on it for years, the purple paint on the ceiling was peeling, revealing spots of white plaster, like stars dotting a night sky.

By the time Omnia arrived at the Nave, it was crowded with people. At one end of the tables sat Allevia, still in the Mourner's Throne that had been carried all the way

31

from the Field of Dreams, and beside her sat Everdean. Every other chair was occupied by a Halibut who had raced into the hall, but there were nowhere near enough chairs for everybody, and other Halibuts who hadn't been as quick stood behind them. At the end of the tables opposite Allevia stood the mass of servants, where the Hereditary Butler would lead them in the feasting.

At a signal from the Butler, Everdean mumbled a few words and the feast commenced.

Everyone reached for the trays, grabbing roast meats gleaming with grease. Those who had found a chair were momentarily crushed by the pressure of the people behind them surging forward to get to the food. No sooner were the meats in hand than the eating began. All over the hall, people crunched and bit. Suddenly the noise was tremendous.

For three hours, the tearing of flesh and the sucking of marrow and the crunching of teeth on bones resounded through the hall. A funeral feast was a tribute to the dead, and the pile of bones at the end of it was the dead person's monument, to be heaped up on the grave and covered with earth. When grass had grown over the top of the pile of bones it would become one of the mounds in the Field of Dreams. Stories were still told of the feast after the death of Everdew the Second, perhaps the best-loved Captain of the House, whose gigantic mound in the field still bore witness to his popularity.

The children took food as well, squeezing between the

adult Halibuts to get to the table, piling dishes with meat and taking them to various parts of the Nave where they sat on the ground and stripped the flesh off the bones and licked their fingers. Each one did their duty, knowing the bones would go into Everwise's mound.

Omnia ate with Evergrow and Sororia and the twins, Artesia and Evesia, and some of her other friends. Eversmart O Halibut was the prankster of the group, with a fondness for shirts with wide stripes. And making a fool of himself. Soon he had stuffed a pair of chicken bones up his nostrils to see who would laugh. Everyone groaned. That only made Eversmart grin. The bones fell out and he went on eating. He had a stupendous appetite and seemed certain to follow the example of his father, Everround Y Halibut, who was one of the great gluttons of the House with a waist to prove it.

Omnia went back to the table with the others to get more. The chewing and sucking and crunching went on. Only Allevia, seated on the Mourner's Throne, seemed to have had her fill, if she had even eaten anything. A full dish stood in front of her, but she didn't touch a morsel. Omnia noticed her sitting with her head tilted against the back of the Throne, apparently staring at the star-spotted ceiling.

Beside her, Everdean sat munching on his food, holding a drumstick or a chop or a rib in each hand within the cuffs of the First Captain's coat, which were now utterly covered in grease from the meats he had eaten. As he ate, he turned from side to side with a startled, birdlike expression on his face, as if no one was more surprised – or more scared – to find himself the possible Captain of the House, or the temporary Captain of the House, or whatever it was that he actually was, and he just couldn't understand how it had happened or what it might mean and what was going to happen next.

The one person who might shed light on the conundrum was Digby, the Hereditary Butler, who stood feasting solemnly in his Butler's coat of dark-green velvet. In one of the pockets of the coat was Everwise's will and when the feast was finished, he would read it out.

Like every Digby who had preceded him, the Hereditary Butler was a small man, and he was old now, with red, rheumy eyes. He was surrounded at the feast by his three UnderButlers, Trimbleby, Withers and Dish. The UnderButlers were all big men, wearing the prune-coloured coats of their office. Next to them stood the Butler's son, the Younger Digby, who would succeed his father when the Older Digby died, and another one of the servants, Tobias Hildegrew. Hildegrew had once been a messenger from a family of messengers, like Cornelius Slinker, but through his natural ability and cheerful nature he had become a friend and assistant to the Younger Digby. The three UnderButlers were jealous of him. Although it wasn't unheard of, they disapproved of a person who had been a mere messenger becoming such a trusted friend of the future Butler, and feared that he would take their place when the Older Digby was gone. They were always making remarks and dropping hints about how unhelpful and difficult he was. But he wasn't unhelpful and difficult. In fact, apart from the UnderButlers, everyone liked him. He was clever and willing, and he was also handsome, with curly, dark hair and a fine, tall figure. Quite a few of the young servant ladies hoped that one day, when Tobias Hildegrew became an UnderButler – as they were sure he must – they would be his UnderButless. Quite a few of the young Halibut ladies secretly dreamed of being Tobias Hildegrew's UnderButless as well, if only Halibuts and servants were ever allowed to marry – which, of course, they were not.

Only the Captain of the House knew the secret of the vast fortune of the Halibuts, and he left a letter about this which only the next Captain would open. This fortune, which the First Captain himself had left behind, was not Everwise's to give away and wouldn't be included in his will. The will that Digby carried concerned Everwise's personal possessions. There was his collection of miniature portraits. There were his silk-lined felt boots, which he had had made in a number of sizes as he grew older, almost as if to spite as many of his fellow Halibuts as possible. And above all there were his puppets, of which he had accumulated a vast number since taking up puppetry as a youth. None of these objects had any particular value, but everyone desired something, not because of what it was worth – a Halibut, after all, wanted for nothing – but because to be left an object in Everwise's will meant that he hadn't thought anybody else more worthy of the gift. Yet the real interest in the will came from the hope that it would solve the great question that Everwise had failed to answer. Who had he preferred as his successor? Who, apart from doddery old Everdean, would be the next Captain of the House?

At length, the eating subsided. People lay slumped in their chairs or stretched out on the floor where they had staggered and fallen, their bellies filled to bursting. It wasn't unknown for people to die from overeating at the feasts in Neversuch House. No one had died this time, but a few candles had been knocked over by people rolling around with their hands on the bellies, starting a number of small fires, one of which scorched a lady's dress before it was put out. Only the most dedicated gluttons of the House, Everround, Everfull V Halibut and his wife, Insatia, and a few others, all sitting in a group not far from Allevia, continued their serious work, but even they showed signs of slowing.

The three UnderButlers pounded on the table for silence and helped the Older Digby climb up, sweeping plates and dishes aside to make way for him.

The Hereditary Butler stood above the crowd. He pulled a document with a large wax seal out of a pocket in his coat and held it up. There was silence in the hall. People who had collapsed on the ground stopped groaning. Even the gluttons stopped chewing.

Digby wiped his greasy fingers on his coat and cleared his throat, much as his great-great-great-great-great-great grandfather had wiped his fingers and cleared his throat just before he read the will of the First Captain at the first such feast, after which he dropped dead on the very table at which he had just eaten. Two other Hereditary Butlers had dropped dead in similar instances, so it wasn't without some anxiety that Digby now proceeded to speak.

'Behold the will!' he cried. He held up the document and showed it slowly to all parts of the Nave so everyone could see it. 'Behold the seal!' he cried, and he showed it again, so everyone could see that the seal was intact. 'I now unseal it!'

He tore off the seal, taking a bit of the paper with it. 'Sorry,' he muttered, and unfolded the thick, crisp document.

Everyone waited.

'Just a minute,' he mumbled, and he fumbled in his pocket for his reading spectacles.

Around the table, eyes rolled.

'That's better. Now, where were we? Ah, yes!' exclaimed the Butler loudly, remembering himself. 'Here are the words of the will of Everwise B Halibut, Tenth Captain of the House.'

He looked at the paper, opened his mouth to speak and frowned.

In the Nave, every eye was on the small man standing on the table in his long, green coat.

'Here are the words of the will,' said Digby again, although something had changed in his voice. A note of doubt, almost disbelief, seemed to have crept in. 'I'm dead now, so I don't—'

'You're not dead!' yelled Everfull, one of the gluttons, spraying chunks of flesh from his mouth. 'Read us the will!'

'This *is* the will!' shouted the Butler back at him. He paused. 'I'll start again.' He cleared his throat. 'I'm dead now, so I don't care what happens. I never liked any of you anyway. You can fight for what you like of my possessions, and whoever gets what they get – gets it.' Digby's frown grew deeper. 'Servants included.'

There was silence.

'That can't be right,' spluttered Everfull, and he clambered on to the table and marched along its length, cracking plates and glasses under his big stomping feet, until he reached the Butler and snatched the paper out of his hand.

He glanced at it and looked up. 'So it is,' he said in amazement.

There was another moment of silence, then someone yelled: 'Everyone for himself!' In an instant, adults and children, Halibuts and servants alike, were pushing, shoving, trampling on each other to get out the door. People who had been groaning with fullness a moment earlier were now on their feet, battling to get out. Everfull jumped off the table, crushing a pair of unfortunate servants beneath him, and waded into the throng, flattening another half-dozen people in his way.

A minute later, the crowd was gone, with only a few injured Halibuts and servants moaning and crawling pitifully out the door. And then they were gone too and the hall was empty, broken plates and smashed glasses and gnawed bones strewn across the table and on the floor.

Or almost empty. At the very end of the table sat Allevia Halibut on her red Mourner's Throne, the only person who remembered that on this day her feet were not supposed to touch the ground. And not far away from her, leaning against the wall, was Omnia.

After the noise of the stampede – the shouts, the groans, the threats, the curses –the Nave was eerily quiet.

Omnia came closer to the table. Allevia's head hadn't moved. It was tilted to one side, resting against the back of the Mourner's Throne, eyes open, as it had been tilted even before the will was read. Maybe, thought Omnia, she had died during the feast and no one had noticed.

Suddenly the old woman turned.

Omnia jumped.

'What are you looking at?' demanded Allevia.

'Nothing,' said Omnia.

The old woman looked at her disbelievingly. 'Aren't you going too? You'll be too late. You won't get anything.'

Omnia shrugged. She didn't know exactly why she hadn't run with the others, she just hadn't. And now that she thought about it, she couldn't imagine what she could possibly want from the possessions of an eighty-seven-year-old man who had had felt boots made for himself in fourteen different sizes.

'What about the puppets?' demanded Allevia, as if she could tell what Omnia was thinking. 'Don't you want a puppet?'

'No,' said Omnia.

'Why not?' said Allevia angrily. 'Everyone else wants one. That's all they've been talking about since he died.'

Omnia didn't reply. The idea of the puppets didn't excite her any more than the boots.

'Come here,' said Allevia, not moving from the Throne. She had white hair that had been set in curls around her head, a flat face and generously spaced teeth. She watched Omnia come closer. 'Let me look at you. That's better. Do I know you? What's your name?'

'Omnia Halibut.'

'Omnia,' repeated the old woman. She thought about it. 'Interesting. I have a question for you, Omnia. Does the name make the person or does the person make the name? Well? What do you think?'

'It sounds like a riddle,' replied Omnia.

'Perhaps it is. I wouldn't have been any older than you when I first heard it and I still haven't made my mind up about it. What's the answer?'

'Perhaps it's both.'

'Both?'

'Perhaps it's neither.'

'That's no answer! Don't try to be clever.' The woman peered at her. She sighed. 'Still, you've got time. Perhaps you'll solve the riddle. Perhaps that's your destiny.'

'I don't believe in destiny,' said Omnia. She sat down beside Allevia. 'I don't believe anything can make you do anything except you yourself.'

'But you're a child,' said Allevia.

'So?'

'Children know very little and what they think they know is almost always wrong.'

'I don't think that's right!'

'Exactly.' Allevia turned her head, looking around at the debris of the feast in the hall. She wore a pair of large diamond earrings and they sparkled in the candlelight. 'What do you think of all this?' She waved her hand at the empty Nave. 'Exactly what Everwise would have wanted. He would have laughed himself sick to see them running out. He did that sometimes, you know, laughed until he vomited. Only at really good jokes. He would have laughed to see this. Right now, where are they? Fighting over his things. Falling over each other to get to the puppets. Bones will be broken on the stairs up to the Hall, mark my words. Bones will be broken and ribs will be cracked. And those who do get up there will be arguing for years over who grabbed what out of whose hand. If Everwise is watching from somewhere, he'll laugh himself sick. He'll laugh so hard he'll die all over again.'

'That's awful,' said Omnia.

'He can't really die again.'

'No, laughing at people fighting over things.'

Allevia shrugged. 'He didn't like them. It's no secret – he said it in his will. Weren't you listening?'

'Then he shouldn't have been our Captain.'

'Oh, he liked them once,' said Allevia. 'It was being the Captain that changed it. That will, he just did it to cause trouble. They'll be squabbling for years. But you know what, Omnia? The biggest curse he left behind him isn't what was in the will, but what wasn't.'

'Is that another riddle?'

'Isn't it obvious? Who'll be the Captain now? Answer me that riddle, eh? Everdean? Will he be the Captain?' Allevia laughed coldly. 'All he cares about is his rocks. Can't wait to get back to them. And if Everdean has to choose someone else to be Captain, would you trust who he'd choose? Think about it. Everdean?'

'We'll find someone,' said Omnia.

'Who? Who's said they want to do it? All they care about is themselves. That's what Everwise saw. As long as nothing stops them doing what they want to do, they don't care about anything else.' Allevia shook her head bitterly. 'You're just a child. Children think everything will turn out right. But things don't. Not always. Quite frequently not, in fact. Oh, it doesn't matter to me. I'm old. But you . . . You're young. How old are you?'

'Twelve and a quarter.'

Allevia nodded. She peered at Omnia, frowning. 'Why did you stay?'

'I just did.'

'You weren't meant to. Everwise told me no one would. Watch, he said, not a single person will remain. The Halibut doesn't exist who won't be carried off with everyone else.'

'Well he was wrong then, wasn't he?'

Allevia stared at Omnia for a moment as if this girl in front of her was the most insolent child she had ever met. Then she started laughing, showing the well-spaced teeth in her mouth.

'He would have liked that answer,' she said through her laughter.

Omnia didn't know that she cared what Everwise would have liked, not after what Allevia had told her about him. And he was dead now anyway, so it didn't matter.

Allevia had stopped laughing. She was peering at Omnia again with that same questioning frown on her face.

'You knew what was in the will, didn't you?' said Omnia.

'They all thought he'd say who should be the next Captain,' replied Allevia, 'but he never did.'

'Not even to you?'

Allevia shook her head. Suddenly her eyes went wide. She clasped Omnia's wrist. She spoke urgently, almost in a whisper. 'Listen to me, Omnia. I saw a bird. On the night after Everwise died. I saw a great black bird!'

'Where?' said Omnia. 'In a dream?'

'I'm not sure. I was looking out the window and I saw it soar above the Great Tower. I saw it by the light of the

43

moon. A great, black bird, Omnia, such as I have never seen before.'

'But it was a dream, is that what you're saying? You dreamed you were looking out the window?'

'I told you I don't know. I'm not sure if I was awake or asleep.' The old woman's grip tightened even more. 'I haven't told anyone else.'

'Why are you telling me?'

'I don't know. What does it mean?'

'I don't know what it means,' said Omnia.

Allevia peered at her. 'Why did you stay, Omnia? Everwise told me no one would. Why didn't you run with the others?'

5

Dawn

The scent woke her. It wafted in under her door, a sweet, sticky, almost sickly aroma, filling the room with a cloying heaviness. Omnia knew where it was coming from. Her brother was up to one of his experiments again in the room next door, earlier than usual. Or perhaps he had been up all night.

She got out of bed and opened a window. The cool, fresh air of dawn rushed in. Her window was high up in the Long South Range at the very edge of the buildings of Neversuch House. Stretching in front of her was a valley and in the distance a lake. Beyond that was a wood, and somewhere beyond the wood, Omnia knew, was the wall around the Halibut estate.

It was a fixed custom that a Halibut never went beyond the wall. This wasn't because nothing was ever needed from the city outside. A population of the size of Neversuch

House, which would have counted as a large village if not a small town, requires all kinds of things. But it was always one of the servants, selected by the Hereditary Butler, who went to arrange them.

This might seem strange, and someone who hadn't grown up in Neversuch House might even think it unfair, but the Halibuts didn't see it that way. From their earliest years they were taught that the world outside was hard, dirty, smelly and tough. People struggled to stay alive there, they were told, and had to work all day to earn enough to feed themselves just so they would have the strength to get up the next day to work again. They were told that only a person who had no alternative would choose to live outside. And since a Halibut did have an alternative – thanks to the vast fortune left by the First Captain – there was no reason for any of them to do that.

The only people who could tell them what it was really like to live in the outside world were the people who came into the House from time to time to marry one of the Halibuts. They never came from the city of Pettifog directly outside, but from far away. They were always young and poor, and generally they were orphans or at least people with only a few elderly relatives who were unlikely to write to them for long. When they married in the House, they took a Halibut name, and thus becoming Halibuts, they never went out of the House again. As the years passed, their memories grew dim and the memories they did have were of their early lives of poverty and hardship in a world they had left ten or twenty or thirty years earlier, while the real world soon changed in ways they themselves wouldn't have recognised.

On the other hand, those who had been born in Neversuch House had never lacked for anything. The saying in the House was that each Halibut was like a Prince or Princess in their realm.

Each family of Halibuts could live anywhere it chose in the vast collection of buildings that the First Captain had constructed and could have as many rooms for itself as it wanted, provided nobody else already occupied them. Beyond the towers and the halls and the long wings of the buildings where the Halibuts lived were yet more towers and halls and wings that had never yet been inhabited, and there were parts the Captain had built that were even now like undiscovered countries waiting to be explored. There were hundreds of rooms, if not thousands, that had never been opened. Each family could cook for itself or could eat in the Tempered Hall above the kitchens where the Coffiers, the fearsome family of cooks from which the High Chef was always chosen, laboured with a brigade of assistants to produce a never-ending succession of dishes in enormous quantities, much of which went to waste. Waste, of course, wasn't something a Halibut was expected to consider.

As for money, each Halibut could have whatever possessions he or she desired from the outside world. No one counted what one spent compared with another. The order was made, the item arrived, the bill came in and somewhere in the Bright Tower, which housed the Butlery, a clerk made a payment.

You might expect that with such an arrangement greed would have got the better of them and the life of every last Halibut would have been an unending spending spree. But that wasn't the case. If you have ever been in a position to buy everything you want – *everything*, not just a lot of things – and if everyone around you was able to have everything they wanted as well, then you will have quickly discovered a peculiar fact: there isn't so much you want at all. The truth is, when everyone around you can have everything they desire, there isn't much point in having anything.

No, the effect on the Halibuts was somewhat different. Rather than trying to get hold of anything and everything, each Halibut, individually, tended to concentrate on only one thing or another that no one else was interested in. Like Everdean Halibut and his rocks, for example. Or like Omnia's father, Evernear K Halibut, and his butterflies.

Omnia's father had spent his whole life studying the butterflies of the estate and had written a number of lengthy books on the subject illustrated by his own hand. There wasn't a butterfly net, box, jar or tong that he didn't possess. Even the choice of the Long South Range for the family's residence, at the very edge of the buildings of Neversuch House, was a result of his butterfly mania. The valley below the Range was always dancing with butterflies in warm weather, and the wood beyond the lake was home to a whole collection of other species. Omnia's father only had to hang a rope ladder from his library and climb the six storeys down the outer wall of the Range to be among them.

This was one of the most remarkable things about the Halibuts. By the time they were adults, each of them seemed to be obsessed with something different, something that to any other person might have appeared utterly trivial, but which to them was the most important thing in the world. Even those who came into the House from the outside eventually succumbed to the habit.

In their rooms, their towers, their studios, their observatories, their libraries, their laboratories, the Halibuts probed and pondered the subjects that entranced them. It was as if there was something in the air of Neversuch House, if not in the genes of the Halibuts themselves, that drew them, as they grew older, further and further into their own imagined worlds, and further and further from the real one. The real world could be left to the servants. All of this might tempt you to think that the Halibuts lacked ambition. You might think that by the time they were adults, they were incapable of anything useful. But there's another way to look at it. Without either the need or the opportunity to do anything useful, what ambition could they have but for things that were useless?

The only Halibut who lacked this luxury was the Captain of the House. Only the Captain was forced to turn his mind away from his own interest to the interests of others, from his own imagined world to the real one. In any other place, the position of Captain would have been actively fought for. People would have schemed and conspired to seize it for themselves. Such were the Halibuts that the Captaincy wasn't fought for, but actively avoided.

Omnia's brother, Eversmooth T Halibut, was seventeen years old and already the strange tendency of the Halibut adults was starting to take hold of him. In the last year, Eversmooth had developed a startling interest in hair wax. It had started innocently enough, as a dab of wax to smooth down an unruly curl, but it soon began to take the familiar Halibut path to a raging obsession. Now he spent an hour or more each day at the mirror carefully shaping his hair into wisps, waves, fronds, points, spears, spikes, spirals and other intricate shapes and patterns, using a range of waxes and gels. He was impatient to be able to grow a beard and moustache so as to be able to shape them as well. He had begun to invent the gels himself, ordering resins from the Middle East and the saps of rare trees from South America that arrived in aromatic bundles tied up in paper. Glass vessels, test tubes and burners arrived, and he had turned his room into a laboratory, which was always full of the fumes of heated oils. Already he was saying his room wasn't big enough and was talking about finding a bigger space where he could set up the proper laboratory he needed to carry out the great work on hair gels that he had in mind. Omnia feared that fifty years of confecting hair gels lay ahead for her brother. She wondered whether she would ever see him again once he set up his laboratory and disappeared inside.

The sweet, sickly scent wafting into Omnia's room the morning after the funeral feast suggested that he had been up all night working on his latest concoction. He hardly ever slept at night now, and whenever Omnia saw him – which happened less and less frequently – he said that the coolness of night was best for making waxes. Omnia stood at the window and breathed in the freshness of the morning air. And if it hadn't been for the cloying smell coming from Eversmooth's experiment, and the need to get fresh air into her lungs, she probably wouldn't have stood there, and might not even have been awake. In which case, you could say that everything that is about to happen to her is Eversmooth's fault.

But Omnia did stand at the window, and as she breathed the fresh morning air, she looked out. The rays of the rising sun were coming from the other side of the building, throwing the shadow of the Long South Range, with its two tall steeples, far across the valley. Further away, the water of the lake glinted.

Far off, beyond the lake, someone came out of the wood.

Omnia's eyes narrowed. The person was all in black, with a hood over his head, presumably to protect him from the morning chill. But even if the hood hadn't been over his face, Omnia was too far away to have been able to recognise him.

He set off at a trot. A messenger's trot, thought Omnia. And a messenger's cloak.

Omnia frowned. What errand could anyone be running this early in the morning? And if it was someone running an errand, surely at this time he should be leaving the House, not coming towards it.

Or had he been out all night? But if he had, what was he doing coming back through the wood? That was nowhere near the gate in the wall.

Omnia watched the figure trotting around the lake. She had seen Cornelius Slinker leaving the previous day, but he had said he was only going into the city with Everwise's death certificate. He said the Butler had told him to go. She still didn't understand why it couldn't have waited until today. Why did he have to miss the feast in order to deliver it?

If that was Cornelius now, if he had been outside the wall all night, there must have been more to his errand than that! Omnia didn't know where in the city the death certificate had to be deposited, but wherever it was it wouldn't take anywhere near so long to get there and back. Even if it did, that still didn't explain why he hadn't come back through the gate and how he had got over the wall.

The figure trotted away to the right and soon disappeared around the corner of the House of Arches, which adjoined the end of the Long South Range.

The valley was empty again, with the lake glittering in the sunlight.

Omnia stood at the window, pondering what she had just seen and what she should do about it.

Although she didn't know it, Omnia was soon thinking of doing the very thing that would set off the extraordinary events that are about to befall her.

6

The Other Side of the Wood

On the morning after the funeral feast only the most dedicated gluttons of the House turned up for breakfast. Everyone else was still digesting the enormous quantities of meat they had eaten in honour of Everwise. But by lunchtime, the hall was as crowded as ever with hungry Halibuts. Soups, pies, sausages and big bowls of buttered greens arrived in the dumb waiters that came up from the kitchens, unloaded by servers in scarlet tunics. Roast legs of lamb, pork, venison and veal stood ready to be carved. Fried fish arrived in trays with buckets of chips. Jellies, cakes, custards and tarts would be on their way up as well. Every time a dumb waiter opened, a blast of hot air from the kitchen below alerted the diners and everyone would look around to see what had arrived next.

The kitchen of Neversuch House consisted of a series of gargantuan, vaulted chambers that stretched beneath the Great Kitchen Court and the Tempered Hall, the huge dining room where any Halibut could come to eat. It was an underground world of knives and carcases and boiling pots and roasting flesh. The ovens were lit every day before dawn and blazed until night, never completely cooling before they were lit again. Breakfast, lunch and dinner, a vast brigade of chefs, choppers, cutters, slicers, rinsers and washers laboured in the heat under the eye of the High Chef, sending the dumb waiters full of food up to the Hall above.

In the Tempered Hall itself, the ceiling was made of copper, and twice a month a team of twenty-two polishers worked all night to maintain its rich, orangey gleam. It was the largest copper ceiling in the world, but the world didn't realise it because the Halibuts had never let anyone know.

Omnia ate with her friends. The previous night, they had all run to the dead Captain's rooms and they each had a story to tell. The crush had been extraordinary, with Halibuts and servants alike grabbing for whatever they could get. Evergrow, her cousin, had come away with a single left boot, size eighteen. Sororia had got herself one of a pair of miniature portraits of a chihuahua dog, and could have had both, but had given one out of kind-heartedness to an old Halibut who wasn't strong enough to get anything for herself and whom she had found, after the rooms had been stripped, sitting in a corner and crying. Eversmart had crawled through the legs of a crowd in the dead Captain's study to salvage a bottle of dried ink. Artesia and Evesia had made it to the Hall of Puppets and managed to come away with a figure of an evil queen, but then they themselves had fought over it and had torn it apart. Evesia ended up with the body and Artesia with the head. They said that fights had broken out all over the place and just about every other puppet had been torn to pieces as well.

Everyone at the table was amazed just to hear that the twins had made it to the Hall. Everwise's puppets had been the most popular objects and stories were already being told about what had happened on the narrow, steep stairs to the Hall as the crowd surged upwards. Bones had been broken, as Allevia predicted. Eversmart, who was wearing a shirt with wide purple stripes, claimed to know for a fact that three Halibuts and four servants lay gravely ill, in danger of death, from injuries sustained in the crush on the stairs.

'What about you, Omnia?' asked Artesia. 'You haven't told us what you got.'

'I didn't get anything,' replied Omnia.

'Couldn't you get through?'

'No, I didn't go.'

Everyone at the table stared at her.

Omnia shrugged. 'I just didn't.' She still didn't know why she hadn't run with the others after the feast. It was peculiar, now that she thought about it.

'Well, just think what you missed out on!' said Evesia snidely.

Omnia did. All her friends seemed extraordinarily happy with themselves and the objects they had acquired, but as far as she could see, the pieces were useless or broken or torn. It sounded as if just about all of Everwise's possessions had been destroyed in the greedy rush to get hold of them. He would have laughed himself sick, Omnia thought, remembering what Allevia had said to her. People had fought in the Hall of Puppets, they had fought in his study, they had fought in all of his rooms and they would probably go on fighting and arguing over who took what from whom for years to come. And if people had broken bones, or died in the crush, Omnia knew, he would have laughed himself even sicker.

There was silence at the table. Everyone was thinking about what Omnia really had missed out on, just as Evesia had suggested. Suddenly no one seemed to have anything else to say about the useless things they had got or the arguments they had seen or the fights that had broken out over Everwise's possessions.

'Guess what I heard this morning!' said Eversmart, who always had a story to tell or a rumour to spread. 'There's a huge black bird that flew off the Great Tower.'

'Who cares about a bird?' demanded Evesia.

'This was *huge*!'

Omnia stared at him. Eversmart was always making things up and playing pranks, and no one else at the table knew whether to believe him. But Omnia had heard about this bird before. Allevia hadn't dreamed it up after all.

According to Eversmart, three people were known to have sighted the bird, all of whom had been looking out of their windows, for some reason, at around midnight after the feast. They had seen it rise above the Great Tower, turn in the moonlight and glide away into the darkness. Their accounts were so similar, and the size of the bird so exceptional, there could be no doubt they had seen the same creature.

'It was as big as a person!' he claimed.

'There's no bird that's as big as a person,' objected Artesia.

'Yes, there is,' snapped Evesia, merely for the sake of disagreeing with her sister.

Everyone looked at one of the other children sitting at the table to see what he thought. Everright F Halibut was Sororia's brother and was generally regarded as the cleverest boy in the House.

'It must be a condor,' said Everright. 'They're the largest birds in the world.'

'Why would a condor come here?' demanded Evesia.

'Why not?' said Eversmart. He grinned. 'It's good enough for us – why not for a condor?'

'Evertwitch will know what it is,' said Sororia.

Unfortunately, Evertwitch N Halibut, the House's foremost expert on birds, hadn't been one of the three to see it the previous night, otherwise they would certainly have had an identification.

'It might be nesting up there,' said Omnia.

Evergrow looked at her with interest. 'On top of the Great Tower?'

58

Omnia nodded. 'What if it's built itself an enormous nest?'

'It's possible,' said Everright. 'If it's going to nest anywhere, it would be at the top of the Tower.'

A rush of hot air came into the Hall. They looked around. A dumb waiter had opened to reveal trays piled high with slabs of omelette. A dozen Halibuts jumped up and ran across.

'If it's got a nest, there might be eggs up there,' said Eversmart slyly, gazing at the omelettes.

'Eversmart, you're awful!' cried Sororia. 'We've never even seen this bird before and now you want to start eating its eggs.'

Eversmart grinned greedily. 'They must be big. I bet just one of them would feed us all.'

'Eversmart! Don't!'

Eversmart laughed.

Suddenly a small, red-haired girl ran up to the table. It was one of Eversmart's sisters, Augmelia.

'They're going up the Tower!' she cried. 'They're going up! They're going up!'

'To see the bird?' said Omnia.

Augmelia nodded quickly, hopping from foot to foot in excitement. The others looked at her doubtfully. Augmelia was a terrible liar, worse than her brother, and would say almost anything to get attention.

'Augmelia,' said Eversmart, 'is this true?'

'It's true!'

People at other tables were talking to each other excitedly. They were getting up and hurrying out.

'If it's not true, you'll be in trouble.'

'It's true! It's true!'

The children looked at each other. They looked at the people leaving from the other tables. Then they looked at the dumb waiters. Pudding hadn't arrived yet – but they could always come back.

They got up and ran.

What Augmelia had told them wasn't exactly true, but it was close.

There was only one entrance to the Great Tower, through a door off the Silent Cloister, but there was nothing silent about the Cloister today. By the time Omnia and her friends arrived, it was packed with Halibuts who had already heard that someone would be going up the Tower, all eager to see what would happen. Some of them had brought food and were in the process of arranging picnics around the ornamental pool in a corner of the Cloister, the better to enjoy the event. More were arriving all the time.

In the middle of all this stood Evertwitch, a small, slightly stooped man with a habit of turning his head in quick, flighty, birdlike movements. He was accompanied by Digby.

If the giant bird was at the top of the Tower, should they go up there or leave it alone? Evertwitch couldn't decide and various Halibuts were shouting suggestions at him, which wasn't helping. The poor man, more accustomed to sitting by himself in a tree all day trying to get a glimpse of a red-crested clawtail or a sulphur-bellied parakeet, or some equally rare creature, had never been the centre of such attention. His head jerked from one side to the other like a startled goose and he could hardly gather his thoughts.

Omnia glanced at Evergrow and they crept round the edge of the crowd, wondering whether they could slip into the Tower without anyone noticing. But the three UnderButlers, Trimbleby, Withers and Dish, stood resolutely at the entrance in their prune-coloured coats, arms folded, barring the way. No one dared to ask them to move, even though they were supposedly servants and the noisy, squawking Halibuts were supposedly their masters. Omnia looked up. There was a window in the wall of the Tower just above the roof of the Cloister, but a pair of UnderUnderButlers guarded it in case anyone had the idea of climbing up on the roof and sneaking in before Evertwitch issued his opinion.

The opinion was a long time in coming. In fact, the whole thing was too much for Evertwich. He told Digby that he would need to go and consult his books and he ran off, head bobbing. The Halibuts didn't seem to notice or to care if they did. There were picnics happening all over the Cloister amid a generally festive air. Halibuts loved nothing more than an occasion or something that they could pretend was one. They liked to have at least two a month, and more if possible, always accompanied by a feast. The last big occasion – excluding the Captain's funeral, which had been an unexpected bonus – had been Barker's Day, which included a shouting competition in the Echo Walk, and that had been a week previously. The next big one was Planque Day, which involved an ancient game using quoits and antlers, and it would be another whole week until then.

Apart from picnics, nothing was happening in the Cloister. Now that the great bird expert had run off, Omnia couldn't see how anything would. She was getting bored.

She glanced at Evergrow. 'You know, I saw something odd this morning.'

'You didn't see the bird as well?' said Evergrow.

'No. Someone came out of the Mottled Wood. I saw him from my window.'

Evergrow looked disappointed. That didn't sound particularly exciting.

'At dawn.'

'What were you doing up at dawn?'

'Eversmooth was stinking the place out.'

Evergrow nodded in sympathy. He rarely went to visit Omnia at home any more, nor did her other friends, for that very reason.

'That's strange, don't you think?' said Omnia.

'Eversmooth's always stinking the place out.'

'No, seeing someone come out of the Wood at dawn.'

'I don't see why you'd think that would have had anything to do with the bird last night.' said Evergrow.

62

Omnia rolled her eyes. 'I'm not saying it did. I'm just saying it's strange to see someone at that time coming out of the Wood.'

'Maybe he'd been hunting.'

'I don't think so. He hadn't caught anything. He looked as if he was coming back from somewhere.'

'Maybe he was collecting mushrooms or something.'

'I don't think he was carrying anything to put them in.'

'Who was it?'

'I'm not sure.' Omnia hesitated. She had a suspicion, obviously.

'Well, there's probably a perfectly reasonable explanation.'

'Probably,' murmured Omnia.

Evergrow watched her. He knew that look on her face. 'Omnia, what are you thinking about?'

'Nothing.'

Evergrow raised an eyebrow.

'I was just thinking I might go to have a look.'

'For what?'

'For whatever I can find.' Omnia glanced around the Cloister. Apart from the picnics, which were now in full swing, nothing was going to happen here for hours. She glanced questioningly at Evergrow.

Evergrow sighed. 'The Mottled Wood?'

Omnia nodded.

'But it's such a long way!'

*

She threw the end of the rope ladder over the window-sill in her father's library. It tumbled down the side of the wall and then hung, reaching all the way to the bottom six storeys below. One after the other, Omnia and Evergrow climbed down and then headed across the meadow at the foot of the Long South Range. The grass was long and butterflies bobbed and floated around them. They reached the lake, skirted the water and eventually came to the edge of the Mottled Wood.

It was about here that the figure had come out. Omnia turned and looked back at the Range. It was a long, pinkish block in the distance, punctuated by seven rows of windows, its two spires rising above it. She was too far away to make out the rope ladder, but she knew which window was her father's library, twelfth from the left on the sixth floor, and her own room was three windows further along.

She wondered if the person could have seen her watching that morning. Omnia didn't think he could have made out a face at that distance, especially if he was looking into the morning sun. It was only because he had been alone after coming out of the Wood, clearly silhouetted against the green grass of the valley in his dark cloak, that she had been able to see him.

They entered the Wood. Now and then they saw a shape flitting between the trees. Deer lived in here, they knew. They went in deeper. There seemed to be a kind of path and Omnia followed it.

'Do you have any idea what we're looking for?' asked Evergrow.

'No,' said Omnia.

'Then how will we know when we find out?'

Omnia laughed. 'Maybe we won't. Maybe we'll—'

Something went past through the trees and they both jumped. By the time they looked around for it, it was gone.

'Maybe we'll find there's nothing at all,' said Omnia, and they kept going.

They walked for at least half an hour, following the path. Eventually they came to the other side of the Wood. Through the trees, the ancient wall of the estate rose in front of them. It stood five metres high, pale, streaked, half covered in moss. The trees had been cut back from the wall so no one could use them to go over it.

Part of the wall was broken.

A small section had collapsed. Stones lay on the ground. But the collapse must have happened years ago because the wall had been repaired, and the repair itself showed signs of age. The hole in the wall had been plugged with a set of vertical bars, with horizontal bars halfway up and at the top to hold them in place. The bars were rusting and covered with moss, just like the wall itself.

You might think that a hole in the wall would have been quite a discovery, but neither of the children were particularly surprised by what they had found. Neversuch House had been built more than two hundred years earlier and there was hardly a building where something wasn't in the process of breaking. Bricks came loose, statues toppled, corners crumbled, roofs collapsed, and at any one time there was more to be fixed in the vast estate than the masons of the House could manage. Anyone living there was accustomed to seeing the jagged outline of some part of a building that needed work or the evidence of repairs that had been made in the past.

Nor was this the first time that Omnia and Evergrow had seen outside the wall of the House. From its towers and turrets, you could see over the wall to the city far away, where life, they had always been told, was hard, dirty, smelly and tough, and where people had to work all day to earn enough to feed themselves just so they would have the strength to get up the next day to work again. But they had never seen it so close.

The two children walked up to the bars. Beyond a narrow strip of open ground was a row of tall trees, not wild like the trees in the Wood, but carefully cultivated in a line. They couldn't see anything beyond that. As they watched, a squirrel came out of the trees, ran across the open ground and sat twitching in front of them. Then it dashed past them through the bars and disappeared up a tree inside the wall.

Omnia took a closer look at the bars. One had less moss on it than the others. She pulled on it. The bar came loose in her hand, leaving a large gap.

Evergrow pulled one of the other bars to see if it was loose as well, but it didn't budge.

Omnia frowned. Finding that one of the bars could be removed didn't necessarily surprise her. Repairs themselves need repair after a while, and just because this one involved the wall around the estate, that didn't necessarily mean it required immediate attention. After all, no wall, no matter how high, can keep people out of a place if they really want to get in. The First Captain knew it when he ordered the wall to be built and everyone in Neversuch House had known it ever since.

The wall was more of a marker than a barrier, a statement saying: *Here is the estate of Neversuch House. Do not enter.* The true defence of the House wasn't the wall that marked its boundary, but the world that had been created within it. A new face will soon be detected among people who have known each other all their lives. A person unfamiliar with habits as strange as those of Neversuch House will quickly reveal himself unless someone explains a hundred odd things, large and small, every day. In the past, those who had tried to infiltrate the House – and from time to time there had been some – had always been found out. The wall was only a physical manifestation of the stronger, less visible defences that guarded the estate.

But now Omnia and Evergrow were standing in front of a gap in the wall that was big enough for a person to get through. If either of them had wanted to, they could simply have walked out.

Yet they didn't. And in fact, they were barely even tempted, not even to put a foot outside the wall. To understand why, you have to imagine what it was like to grow up as a child inside Neversuch House.

It wasn't only that they had always been told that the world outside was hard, dirty, smelly and tough. After all, you might want to go somewhere even if you know it's going to be a horrible place, just to see what it's like. Even more than this, it was that they had also been taught that a true Halibut, a good Halibut, wouldn't want to go out there – that to go out there would somehow betray what it meant to be a Halibut – just as you might be taught that a good person doesn't lie or hit or steal. Not stepping outside the wall, even if they could, was as natural to them as it might be natural to you not to take your best friend's book, or ring, or money, just because they've forgotten it for a moment and would never know who stole it.

Omnia replaced the bar. She stood for a moment, thinking.

Finding a segment of the wall that had crumbled wasn't a surprise, nor was finding that the repair of the wall itself had broken. But someone *had* come out of the wood that morning, and if they *had* come from outside – which was the question, of course – it seemed obvious that they would have used this crumbling section of wall to enter the House.

And if they had used it once, it was possible that they would use it again – which would be quite interesting to know, to say the least.

She looked around and found some dry leaves. She raised the loose bar and forced a couple of leaves in where it slotted into the rock at the base of the wall.

*

68

The next morning, as the pungent aroma of her brother's latest gel wafted through her room at dawn, Omnia was already up and watching. She didn't see anyone come out of the Wood.

Later, she went to check the wall. The leaves were still in place, in exactly the same position as she remembered leaving them.

But merely by going back, Omnia had sealed her fate. As she carefully checked the bar to see if it had been moved, she didn't stop to think that behind her, among the trees, were a hundred hidden places from which a pair of eyes might be watching her.

7

The First Extraordinary Event (or Two)

The Hall of Leaning stood not far from the Purple Nave. Its walls were lined with bookcases, a podium with a lectern was at the front of the Hall and below the podium were rows of desks. Everything leaned, the podium and the lectern and the bookcases and the desks, just as the name of the Hall suggested.

Yet it should never have been called the Hall of Leaning at all. The mason who carved the name over the entrance of the Hall, which was intended by the First Captain for the education of the children of the House, had forgotten one important letter.

It was a mistake any mason could have made, particularly one who wasn't much of a scholar and had a hundred other things to do in those days of frenzied work when the House rose from its foundations. And it was a mistake any foreman could have failed to notice when checking a

70

mason's work, particularly when he had a hundred other things to check. Or perhaps he did notice it, and decided it wasn't so important, not in comparison with everything else that still needed to be done, and surely people in the future would realise it was an error and would correct it if they wanted to.

But the Hall was one of those buildings the First Captain prepared for future generations, when the population of Neversuch House would have grown. His own six children didn't need such a large space for their lessons, nor did his grandchildren or their children, and it was only in the generation after that that the building came into use. By then, the First Captain was long dead, and so was his original assistant, the first Digby, and everyone knew the place as the Hall of Leaning because that was what the name over the entrance said.

No one could work out, when they finally opened it up and went inside, why nothing seemed to lean. The floor was perfectly level. So the workmen of the House were asked to fix the mistake, and when they were finished, the floor sloped noticeably from one side to the other and every item of furniture in the Hall leaned forwards or backwards or sideways, depending on its position, and the larger pieces were inclined to fall when accidentally disturbed. The bookcases especially, being so tall and narrow, were likely to topple, and extracting a book in the Hall of Leaning was an operation to be carried out with great care if you didn't want to find yourself with a thousand books crashing down around you, not to mention the bookcases themselves, which were weighty enough to crush a small child to death and do considerable damage to a larger one.

As for what happened within the Hall of Leaning, if you compare it with the schools most children go to, you'll probably think the education at Neversuch House was an unusual affair. After each child – Halibut and servant alike – had been taught to read and write and perform simple mathematical tasks with the aid of fingers, toes and a collection of small pebbles, the two groups went their separate ways. The servant children were educated in the tasks that they would perform when they were grown up, which was usually the work that their parents and grandparents and great-grandparents had performed before them. The Halibut children, on the other hand, were free to learn anything else – or nothing else – according to their preferences. If they wanted to learn, the Hall of Leaning was at their disposal, with all the books in its bookcases and lessons given by the older Halibuts. If they didn't want to learn, there were the meadows and the woods and the swamps of the estate outside, which had their own lessons to teach.

You might imagine that as a result not a single child would ever have turned up to the Hall of Leaning. Yet people are peculiar creatures, whether adult or child, and this wasn't the case. More often than not, a good number of desks in the Hall were occupied with children reading or listening to the lesson that was in progress. But if you compare them with the lessons in the schools most children go to, you might not recognise them as lessons at all. They were more like lectures, or speeches, or even songs and exhibitions and theatrical performances, depending on the nature of the older Halibut who was giving the lesson and his or her particular obsession.

Any adult Halibut could give a lesson on anything, no matter how obscure or how little its educational benefit. Everwise B Halibut, in the days before he became Captain of the House, had given puppet shows. His nephew, Everhale U Halibut, who still regularly climbed the steps to the podium at the front of the hall, normally just told a string of jokes about whatever had happened to him that morning. Everhale was an extreme example and was strongly discouraged by Pedagogia Halibut, the leading poet of the House, who was also the self-appointed and unofficial headmistress of the school. But Pedagogia had no right to keep anyone away, even if she wanted to, because no one had ever officially appointed her to be headmistress, and so she had no more power to select the 'teachers' – if that is even the right word for them, which is questionable – than anyone else.

So the Halibut children were exposed to an unending succession of 'lessons' – if that is the right word, which is even more questionable – about subjects you wouldn't find on any school curriculum. Very little of what went on in the Hall did anything to equip a child with the skills to deal with the real world, which is what most schools try to do. But if you think about it, like so many things in Neversuch House, what would have made no sense at all to someone who had not grown up in the House made perfect sense to those who had. Since the adults of Neversuch House didn't have to deal with the real world, there would have been no point in equipping the children of the House to do that either.

On the other hand, since most of their teachers had never even been outside the House, and knew nothing but the House, and were interested in nothing but the House, the House was what most of the lessons were about – which is what the children *did* need to know. Although not necessarily in as much detail as they got.

As the years passed, each subject about the House was split into sub-subjects, and into sub-sub-subjects, and into smaller subjects still. The architecture of the House, its history, its fauna, its flora, its weather patterns, its soils, its rocks, its lakes, its woods – each generation was brought up learning these subjects, each generation spent its life studying them, so this is what each generation taught in turn to the generation that came next.

Thus it was that Omnia Halibut, two days after having discovered the barred gap in the wall of the estate and having checked the leaves to make sure the bar was undisturbed – not just on the first morning after she had left them but on the second morning as well – found herself sitting in a lesson being given by Everfine D Halibut on the shadows thrown by the buildings of the House.

Everfine, a thin gentleman with different coloured eyes – one blue, one grey – had set himself the task of measuring, mapping and recording the shadows thrown by each architectural component of the House – tower, wall, spire, roofline, corner – by hour of the day and by day of the year. Forty years after starting, working his way systematically across the House, he had barely covered a tenth of the buildings and had begun to realise that his entire lifetime would suffice to finish only a fraction of the great work. He was looking for someone to carry it on, and sometimes, when she saw him glancing at her, Omnia imagined that Everfine hoped she might be the one. Omnia didn't think so! Shadows were all very well, but they were here now, gone later. Just like Everfine himself would be, thought Omnia with a secret smile.

Omnia's mind wandered – initially, to the question of why she was sitting here listening to this in the first place. As she gazed out the window, she saw a pigeon fly past. That reminded her of the great, black bird everyone was talking about.

There had been no fresh sightings of the creature, and yet a growing number of people were insistent that they had seen it on the night of Everwise's funeral. So consistent was their description that they must have seen *something*. Perhaps it was up there right now at the top of the Great Tower, brooding on a giant nest. After much deliberation and careful study of his books, Evertwitch, the bird expert, had been persuaded to lead an expedition to the top of the Tower, and equipment was being prepared, nets, ropes, even a gigantic cage which would be taken up in pieces to be assembled once the bird was netted and which would then be lowered down the side of the Tower by rope.

Omnia tried to imagine Evertwitch stalking the monstrous creature with a net. He was a birdwatcher, not a birdcatcher. The idea of Evertwitch trying to catch a giant bird at the top of a soaring tower seemed to have the makings of a terrible accident – and not for the bird.

It was the image of this that Omnia was thinking about – or trying not to think about – when she became aware that her name was being called.

She looked back at the podium. Everfine was holding a large canvas scroll, partially unfurled, on which he had meticulously mapped the seasonal outlines of the shadow thrown by the House of Arches in a series of different coloured lines according to a system he had invented himself.

'Omnia, please come up and hold the other end so we can all see.'

Omnia glanced at Artesia and rolled her eyes. There was no *way* she was going to take over the work from Everfine when she grew up. Artesia giggled.

'Omnia? Come on, everyone's waiting . . .'

Everyone couldn't care less, as far as Omnia could tell. Still, she got up to go to the podium.

'Thank you, Omnia. Now just come up and—'

She felt something brush past her. There was a tremendous crash.

Everfine's voice had stopped. A shocked hush had come over the Hall.

The chair on which Omnia had been sitting only a few seconds earlier was smashed to splinters. Broken fragments of a stone tile were scattered across the floor.

Omnia looked up. A square of blue sky was visible through a hole in the roof. A shadow flitted across the hole – a cloud blowing across the sun, perhaps – and was gone.

But by now everyone was gathering around and the silence in the Hall was turning into a typical Halibut uproar. There were children on every side, all desperate to inform Omnia what would have occurred if Everfine hadn't happened to call her up just when the tile fell. As if Omnia needed anyone to tell her. Nothing more would have been left of her head than of the chair which lay in splinters at her feet.

'I've been saying it for years!' cried Pedagogia, standing with her hands on her hips. 'We need to fix the roof. Someone's going to be killed! I've been saying it for years!'

Pedagogia, whose poetic nature made her prone to exaggeration at times of high emotion, had been saying no such thing for no such time. She had, however, wondered once or twice whether the roof should be checked for safety. That was close enough, given what had just happened.

A number of people – Halibuts and servants – had hurried in from outside when they had heard the crash of the falling tile. 'I've been saying it for years!' Pedagogia exclaimed to each new arrival, stoking the uproar in the Hall, which drew even more people in.

The uproar grew greater. Soon people would be arriving with picnic baskets to view the chaos unless someone did something to quieten the crowd.

At last, a calming voice was heard. 'Ladies and gentlemen! Please. *Please*. There's no need to panic.' It was Tobias Hildegrew, the servant who was the friend of the Butler's son. He had come in from outside like the others.

The shouting died down. People gazed at his handsome face, relieved that someone seemed to know what he was doing. Tobias always seemed so steady and self-assured. There was no one who was more able to reassure a crowd of overexcited Halibuts.

'Let's have some calm,' he said. 'That's better. All right. Now, first things first. Is anyone hurt?'

'Not this time,' said Pedagogia. 'But I've been saying it for years! This roof is dangerous.'

'Yes, Miss Pedagogia. Quite right. We'll have to get it fixed.'

'I mean it!'

'I agree. But is anyone hurt? That's the first thing.' Hildegrew knelt beside Omnia. 'Omnia, are you all right?'

Omnia nodded.

'Sure?'

'Yes, I'm sure.'

'I called her up at the critical moment,' said Everfine.

'To show the shadows. Omnia, one might say the shadows saved your life.'

Forget it, Everfine, thought Omnia. I'm not going to do it.

Tobias looked up at the roof. 'That was a lucky escape, Omnia. A tile! Thank goodness you weren't sitting there when it fell.'

Omnia glanced up at the roof as well. Yes, lucky. More than lucky. An extraordinary event. Two extraordinary events. First, that a tile should just have happened to fall exactly on the spot where she had been sitting all morning. Second, that she shouldn't have been sitting there when it hit.

8

An Invitation

An unfortunate accident, that was the general opinion about the event at the Hall of Leaning. Not merely unfortunate, but freakish, in the opinion of Albert Gondolier, the Chief Mason and head of the Gondolier family, who had been masons to the Halibuts since the days of the First Captain.

Albert Gondolier climbed a long ladder up to the roof, followed by four of the most experienced masons under his command. One after the other, they examined the roof carefully and an hour later were utterly at a loss to explain how a tile could have come loose from an area of the roof where every other tile seemed to be firmly fastened, and when all the loose tiles elsewhere on the roof – and there were a lot of them – had failed to be dislodged. They examined it again and another hour later there was still no answer. So Albert Gondolier filled in a detailed report which he gave to one of the masons, who climbed down from the roof and took it to Digby, the Butler, who gave it to one of the UnderButlers, who gave it to the Master Filer, who gave it to one of the clerks in the Butlery, who filed it away under 'Freak Accidents' in one of the dusty boxes in one of the dusty rooms where the bills, invoices, receipts and reports of Neversuch House had been filed for over two hundred years. Then the Chief Mason watched as one of the other masons fixed the hole in the roof, putting an identical tile in the identical spot and fastening it in the identical way in which the first tile had been fastened until it freakishly came loose and plummeted on the chair where Omnia Halibut had been sitting only two seconds before it fell.

And that was the end of the matter. Albert Gondolier and the masons climbed down from the roof and marched off, taking their ladder with them. Everyone else in the House was much more interested in the expedition to the top of the Great Tower to catch the black bird than in the crashing of a piece of masonry, which must have happened somewhere in the House every single day, although not necessarily with as nearly fatal a result. The expedition was due to take place later that afternoon. And in the evening, everyone was still more interested in the expedition, even though it had found nothing at all, not a bird, not a nest, only the droppings of the pigeons that habitually roosted on the Great Tower and which were cleaned away each year before Landing Day, when the Captain of the House was supposed to climb to the top.

The next morning, Omnia walked into the Hall of Leaning and pulled a chair up to the desk where she had sat the previous day. She sat down, ignoring the looks of the children around her.

'You're not going to sit there, are you?' asked Evergrow eventually.

Omnia looked at him in surprise. 'Can you think of a safer place?'

'But that's where the tile fell!'

'Exactly. And now it's been fixed. When was the last time anyone fixed any other tiles up there?' Omnia glanced at the roof and then looked meaningfully at all the other Halibut children who were staring at her.

They looked up at the roof as well.

Evergrow got up and dragged a desk across until it was right next to Omnia.

Then Artesia, Omnia's friend, dragged another desk across, followed by Evesia, Omnia's enemy. Followed by everyone else. Soon every desk that was occupied was clustered around Omnia in the middle of the sloping floor.

Pedagogia arrived and told everyone to take their desks back. But no one moved. And as Everjay M Halibut arrived to give a talk about the acorn-gathering habits of the squirrels that lived on the roofs of the Midges Mansion – exemplified by a number of half-nibbled acorns he had brought along for display – Pedagogia herself inched closer to the mass of children and ended

82

up standing just behind them, unconsciously leaning forward to get as close as she could to the spot where Omnia was sitting.

That afternoon, Omnia went back to the Wood to check the gap in the wall once more. She hadn't been there since the previous morning and had more or less given up expecting to find that the leaves had been disturbed. After all, there was nothing to show that the person she had seen emerging from the Wood early in the morning after Everwise's funeral had used the gap or had even been aware of it. She had almost convinced herself that even if it was Cornelius Slinker, he had probably been doing something perfectly understandable, collecting birds' eggs, for example, or gathering mushrooms, or doing a hundred other things a person might do in a wood at daybreak. And the fact that a bar in the wall was loose didn't prove anything. Things like that happen when something is neglected for years, as Omnia knew.

Yet Omnia did go back to check, telling herself that this would be the last time. And if she hadn't, it is very likely that the series of extraordinary events that befell her would have stopped right here, before they had barely even begun, and that everyone would have always believed that the falling tile in the Hall of Leaning really was just a freak accident, Omnia included. But then this wouldn't be much of a story – certainly not enough for a book – so I wouldn't have written it down and you would never have heard of

Omnia Halibut at all but would be reading something else now instead, although it probably wouldn't be as exciting and as almost-unbelievable as the story which is about to unfold. Every word of which, by the way, is true, and every event in which is real, as real as Neversuch House itself.

And you're probably wondering, by now, how it is that I know about all these things, and even about Neversuch House, which I suspect you had never heard of until you picked up this book. I suppose I could invent some explanation, although I've never been very good at making up stories. I could say I heard it from an old lady as she lay dying and I never found out her name. Or I read it in a diary that I found hidden in a dusty attic which I was exploring one day when I had nothing better to do. But the truth is stranger than anything I could make up, as truth often is. It would be a whole story in itself, and who's to say that one day I won't tell it? But since I've already started on the history of the extraordinary events that befell Omnia Halibut at the age of twelve and a quarter – the first of which has already befallen her, and which are more than enough of a story in themselves – I think we ought to continue with that.

So to return to Omnia . . . She does go back to the wall that afternoon. And although the leaves at the bottom of the bar are undisturbed, just as they have been on each of the previous occasions that she has come to check, there is something new there. A scrap of paper, folded up and tucked in among the stones.

Omnia unfolds it. The ink on the paper has run slightly because of the dew, but the words are legible. There are only four of them.

Look to your left.

Omnia looks. At first up into the trees, thinking there might be something high in the branches. Only then does she look down. And she sees them. Words. Only a couple of metres away, scratched in the ground.

*IF YOU WANT TO KNOW WHAT REALLY
HAPPENED AT THE HALL OF LEANING
COME TO THE TOP OF THE SLATE TOWER
AT SIX O'CLOCK TOMORROW MORNING*

9

The Studio in the House of Arches

Omnia walked quickly. The atmosphere in the Wood felt different now. Sinister, dark. Someone had discovered that she had been at the wall. Perhaps even seen her.

She broke into a run.

At last, she was out of the trees. She stopped. Ahead of her was the bulk of the Long South Range with its two spires, and adjoining it the House of Arches, named for a series of huge, semicircular arches that looped along the top of the building. Beyond them rose the other turrets and towers of the House.

The words went through her mind. What really happened at the Hall of Leaning . . . What was that supposed to mean? She knew what happened at the Hall of Leaning, didn't she? A tile had fallen. An accident. Unfortunate. Freakish. But an accident, surely.

What else was there to say about it? And why would

someone who had discovered that she had been at the wall want to tell her?

The message instructed her to come to the Slate Tower. On the jagged skyline of the House, the Slate Tower was second in height only to the Great Tower itself. Omnia could see the outline of its pointed top, far off in the distance.

As far as Omnia was aware, no one lived in the Slate Tower or had used it for years. It was a round tower with a turret and it was entirely covered in grey-greenish slate, from which its name derived. Its windows were always dark, some shuttered, some open and blank from which the shutters had torn away. It had fallen into disrepair and from time to time, on stormy nights, one or two of its slates would come loose and plummet to the ground.

Why there? If someone had something to tell her, why couldn't he or she tell her somewhere else?

Omnia walked around the edge of the lake. She stopped and gazed at the turret of the Slate Tower again, rising high in the distance. She realised that she didn't know how to get there. The Slate Tower was in a remote area of the House where there was a complicated series of tiered wings and tall lodges with pitched roofs overlooking deep court-yards and twisting alleys. Where exactly the entrance was, she couldn't say.

Not that she was necessarily going to go there. Just because the message invited her to go, she didn't have to do it. Why the Slate? And why six in the morning? And how did the person who left the note know that she would come back and find it? And then why write the actual message in the ground? It seemed suspicious, to say the least.

But what *had* really happened at the Hall of Leaning? The words had piqued Omnia's curiosity. If it wasn't what it seemed, she wanted to know.

And yet the top of the Slate Tower, all by herself, at six in the morning . . .

Well, she could at least find out how to get there. Finding out didn't mean anything. It didn't mean she was actually going to go, did it?

Who could tell her? She needed someone who wouldn't pry, wouldn't ask any questions, wouldn't demand to know why she was asking and then try to tell her what to do. Someone who would tell her how to get to the Slate Tower and not think twice about it.

Omnia's eye rested on the House of Arches. She nodded to herself.

They were a pair, Evermay L Halibut and Everset E Halibut, and it was hard to imagine either one of the two friends without the other. They shared a studio high at the very top of the House of Arches, where enormous windows provided an abundance of light, and there, chattering incessantly to each other and to anyone else who happened to drop in, they did their work.

Evermay was a painter who produced vast canvases of

celebrated episodes from the history of Neversuch House, daubing colour at a frenetic speed and sometimes finishing a painting a day. His canvases were stacked three-high and eight-deep on special shelves around the walls of the studio. Everset, on the other hand, was a sculptor who worked in the tiniest miniature, gazing through the lenses of ever-increasingly powerful microscopes, and might labour on the same carving for months, whittling and paring with infinite patience. A green porcelain matchbox on his desk contained his entire life's work.

They were murmuring to each other as usual when Omnia came in. Everset, wearing a dark suit with a meticulously knotted tie, was hunched over his microscope, while Evermay was striding around in a paint-splattered smock and crimson cravat, wild-haired, red-faced, throwing paint at an enormous canvas. He was at work on a new painting. Already there was a turbulent, stormy sky daubed across the background, a group of men bursting heroically out of a door and the figure of a gigantic bird rising into the air, looking something like a monstrous pigeon, its eye burning red, its beak open, its enormous wings throwing a shadow over the entire scene.

Evermay turned, paintbrush in hand, not at all surprised to find someone standing behind him. 'Omnia, what do you think? I call it: *Expedition to the Top of the Great Tower to Snare the Black Condor*.'

'I've suggested he change the title,' remarked Everset, gazing down the lens of his microscope. 'He should put

Mystery in it. Or *Mysterious*. Call it the *Mysterious Condor*, Evermay. People love a title like that. They'll go crazy for it.'

'That's what you always say.'

'I'm only trying to help.'

'If I listened to you, every painting I do would be a *Mystery*. A bit like your sculptures.' Evermay laughed. 'They're so small they're a mystery to us all.'

The sculptor smiled. 'Thank you, Evermay. I take that as a compliment.'

'What do you think, Omnia?' demanded the painter.

Omnia frowned. 'I don't think you need to have *Mystery* in the title. Or *Mysterious*. It's not very original.'

'Exactly!' said Evermay. 'Now look at it, Omnia. Forget the name, look at the work! Well? What do you think? Is it a masterpiece?'

Omnia gazed at the canvas. 'Is this meant to be yesterday's expedition?'

'Of course,' said Evermay.

Omnia glanced at Everset, who shrugged, a movement purely of his shoulders, so as not to disturb by even a fraction of a millimetre the position of his hands. Even when he carved, the movements of his fingers were so slight that you could hardly see them.

'It wasn't cloudy yesterday,' said Omnia.

'That's for effect,' replied Evermay.

Omnia frowned. 'That's not Digby, is it?' she asked, although she knew that it was. Unmistakable in the green velvet coat of the Hereditary Butler and with rheumy eyes almost popping out of his head, Digby was shown leaping up the last of the stairs, clutching a huge net, leading the men who were bursting onto the roof of the Great Tower. Yet Digby hadn't climbed the Tower yesterday, nor had he climbed it for years, being too arthritic to get to the top. He had sent the three UnderButlers along with Evertwitch and half a dozen UnderUnderButlers to carry the nets and pieces of the cage to catch the bird – which, incidentally, hadn't been there when they arrived, which was another point on which the painting differed from reality.

'Omnia,' said Evermay, 'what are future generations going to think if they knew our own Butler wasn't there at this crucial moment in our history? Who wants to see three UnderButlers and a bird-watcher?'

'And the bird?' said Omnia.

'Who wants to see the Hereditary Butler charging out onto an empty roof?'

'What would be the point of that?' asked Everset from his desk.

'What *would* be the point?' said Evermay.

'Make him look like a fool,' murmured Everset.

'An idiot,' said Evermay.

Omnia gazed doubtfully at the canvas.

'*This* is an event,' said Evermay proudly. '*This* is something to capture for posterity.'

'We're artists,' murmured Everset, still staring down the microscope. 'Not historians.'

'Exactly. We're artists. A painting must capture the meaning, Omnia, not just the appearance. The appearance is nothing. The meaning is all.'

'And what *is* the meaning?' inquired Omnia.

'Can't you see? Look! The stormy sky! The bird throwing its shadow! Omnia, can't you see the meaning?'

'Maybe she'll be able to see it better when it's finished,' said Everset.

'She can see it now. It's obvious. How much more obvious can it be?'

'Maybe it's too obvious,' said Omnia. 'If you just explained it a bit . . .'

'Omnia, the bird is a sign.'

'Of what?'

'Exactly! Why has it come now? Why has it suddenly appeared?'

Evermay gazed fiercely at Omnia to see if she understood. Everset had taken his eyes off the microscope and was looking at her as well.

'Why?' asked Omnia quietly.

'Who knows?' cried Evermay, raising his hands dramatically in the air.

'He's an artist,' said Everset. 'He asks the questions, he doesn't answer them.'

'Look at the painting, Omnia! Are you saying the bird's not a sign? See the wings? See the shadow? See how it falls over everything? See? Over the whole House. Even in the background.'

'She'll see it better when it's finished,' said Everset.

'She can get the idea already!' said Evermay, and he dipped a brush in black paint and strode along the canvas, smearing it energetically to deepen the shadow over the buildings in the background.

Omnia watched him. 'Do you really think the bird is a sign?'

'Look at the painting!' cried Evermay again. He slapped more black paint on the canvas. 'Look at the shadow! The painting doesn't lie.'

Omnia glanced at Everset.

'An artist knows,' said Everset. 'An artist knows, even if he can't say why.'

Omnia stepped forward. She pointed at the dark outline of a turret in the background of Evermay's painting. 'Is that the Slate Tower?'

'Of course it is,' said Evermay.

'How do you get there?'

'Through a house somewhere.'

'The Blue House,' murmured Everset, his eyes on his microscope once more.

'The Blue House then,' said Evermay. He had no head for details. He prided himself on thinking in terms of the grand sweep, grand gestures, like his paintings. Everset was the one for trivia.

'You go to the top of the Blue House,' said Everset. 'Open the door and there's a walkway between two court-yards. Cross the walkway and you're there.'

'Be careful,' said Evermay. 'You won't be far from the Herd of Hounds. You wouldn't want to fall.'

'Evermay! Don't scare the girl.'

The painter chuckled.

'How do you get to the Blue House?' asked Omnia.

'Oh, that's easy,' said Evermay. 'Up the Reaper's Stairs. Go to the top and you can't miss it.'

'Go to the top and go left,' said Everset. 'You'll see a narrow arch. Go under that, go left again. You'll find yourself in a small square. The Blue House is there.'

'How will I know it?'

'You'll know it. If you don't know it, you're in the wrong place.'

'And the Reaper's Stairs . . . ?' said Omnia.

'You know the Minor Terrace?' asked Evermay.

Omnia shook her head.

'The Granite Arch?'

'It's nowhere near the Granite Arch,' said Everset impatiently. 'That's the other side of the House. Omnia, do you know the Echo Walk?'

'Of course.'

'Go down the Echo Walk and at the end of it you'll come to a small set of stairs. Go to the top and you'll soon come to an open area. That's the Minor Terrace. On one side are some trees.'

'Oaks!' cried Evermay.

'Pines,' said Everset. 'They're on one side – you go to the other. From there you'll see the Reaper's Stairs.'

'And that's it?'

'That's it.'

Omnia repeated the directions to make sure she had understood them. Everset nodded into the microscope.

'And the Tower?' asked Omnia. 'Is it open?'

'Is it open, Everset?' said Evermay, still deepening the shadow in the painting.

Everset shrugged, one of those shrugs that left his hands completely still. 'No idea. Haven't been there for years. No one lives there. Could be locked.'

But it wouldn't be locked, thought Omnia, if someone had told her to come to the top.

Not that she had definitely made up her mind to go. She was only finding out in case she decided to.

Everset looked up at her with interest. 'Why do you ask? Are you planning on going there?'

Omnia shrugged. 'Not necessarily.'

10

At the Top of the Slate Tower

Omnia wrapped a blanket around her shoulders against the chill. Light came from under the door to Eversmooth's room, together with the aroma of his latest concoction. She slipped quietly along the corridor, down the stairs and out of the Long South Range.

It was still dark. The clocks of the House had chimed five o'clock not long before. Omnia crossed the square in front of the Long South Range to the Gabled Lodge and took a shortcut through its corridors. From behind the closed doors came the snorings and snufflings and mufflings of slumbering Halibuts. Omnia came out the other side and kept going, more stairs, more corridors, more courtyards. In the Great Kitchen Court she saw smoke rising from the chimneys of the bakery and the cool air carried the scent of fresh-baked bread. Looking up, she saw lights in the windows of the Tempered Hall, which was being prepared

96

for breakfast. A kitchen hand came out of a doorway in front of her carrying a tray of pig livers. Another kitchen hand came past, pushing a wheelbarrow full of gutted fish.

Omnia left the Court by a set of stairs that took her to the Pale Octangle, then another set of stairs that took her close to the Bright Tower. She made her way through the buildings clustered round it. Then she was at the Long Promenade, and at the end of that she was back among a maze of buildings. After a few turns she came to the Echo Walk, which cut through the buildings like a long, snaking tunnel.

The Echo Walk was one of the peculiar structures the First Captain had had built in the House almost as a form of mischief, like the Hatted Belfry and the Hall of Murmurs, or the great Bracketball Courts that he had constructed even though it would be another fifty years before the game of Bracketball was invented. The masons had put carvings into the buildings for the same reason, animals with human faces, people watching with puzzled expressions who would suddenly loom out at you in the most unexpected places and make you jump with fright. The Walk had inward-sloping walls and an arched roof that formed a kind of tube, built to magnify sound and exaggerate every echo. On Barker's Day, the winner of the shouting competition was the one who could make the echoes last longest, and the loudest Halibuts competed with gusto.

As she went through it, Omnia's footsteps resonated to and fro along the tube, overlapping with each other until they created a continuous, thundering chain of noise. Then she came out into the open and suddenly the only sound, once more, was the quick, light tap of her footsteps. Following Everset's instructions, she took the stairs at the end of the Walk, headed away from the trees at the edge of the Minor Terrace and found a wide set of stairs on the other side, flanked by a pair of figures with long reaper's scythes. One of the sculptures showed a young man in the full flush of health, the other an old man with skeletal head and hands.

Omnia went up the stairs. She turned left at the top, under the arch and left again, and found herself in a small square with four tall, narrow houses rising around it. She understood why Everset had said she would know which was the Blue House, and if she didn't, she wouldn't be in the right place. Each of the houses had wide bands of coloured tiles set into their bricks. The one with blue tiles was on her right.

Inside, the house was ornately decorated, walls, pillars, floors and ceilings all covered in materials in different shades of blue. Everset had told her to go to the top. Omnia went quickly up the stairs, past four landings. Then there was a yellow door and she opened it.

A wind hit her, blowing straight into her face. In front of her was a long stone walkway, and at the other end of the walkway rose the Slate Tower. Its windows – some shuttered, some open and dark – rose in a long, dizzying line high into the sky.

Omnia set off across the walkway. On either side of her, far below, was a courtyard, and beyond the courtyards, in the grey of the dawn light, Omnia could see a jumble of roofs. Far off on her right was a huge court, much bigger than the ones immediately below her. She could see only its opening. A mist seemed to have settled down there, obscuring anything below the very top.

Omnia wondered whether that was where the Herd of Hounds lived. It was somewhere out here, Evermay had said, and then Everset had told him not to try to scare her, so Omnia didn't know if they were serious. According to the stories Omnia had been told, the Herd were the descendants of a single pair of dogs that had been trapped in a courtyard when it had been mistakenly sealed off by the First Captain's masons. For more than two hundred years they had multiplied and no one knew how many there were. Hundreds perhaps, or thousands. They lived on meat that was thrown into the court and from birds that foolishly flew too low and from water that collected when it rained. And from the bodies of people who had gone to try to see them, according to the stories, and had fallen in from the top.

Omnia listened. Perhaps there was a sound of baying coming from the direction of the huge court. A kind of doggy howling. Or perhaps it was only the wind in her ears.

She looked up again. The sky was getting light now. The message had instructed her to be at the top of the Slate Tower at six.

Omnia crossed the walkway. At the other end, the door of the Tower was open.

Inside was a spiral staircase. Omnia climbed. Light came into the staircase from long, narrow shafts. The stairs kept going in a smooth, spiralling curve, always five or six steps visible in front of her and looking just the same as the last five or six she had climbed. Her legs began to ache. Finally there was a doorway ahead and Omnia got to the top. She hesitated for a moment, poked her head out, and then stepped outside.

The wind was even stronger up here. Omnia found herself at the base of the turret, which rose higher still to its point. A narrow walkway led around the base with a waist-high parapet at its edge. Beyond it, Omnia could look down on virtually the entire House and the estate all the way to the wall, not only over the buildings where the Halibuts had their homes, but over the dark, jumbled mass of the Warren, the area about a mile further north in the estate where the servants lived. The Warren had grown out of the camp where the army of workers had lived in the days when the House had been built, and it was a fixed custom that no Halibut ever went there. But it was barely visible now to Omnia because of the mist, which lay low to the ground and seemed to have grown thicker. Immediately below her, the House was covered in a blanket of greyish fog, its spires and turrets poking through the top. The Great Tower soared out of it into the clear air, the only structure taller than the Slate.

There didn't appear to be anyone waiting for her. Omnia looked up at the turret again, almost as if she expected to find someone clinging to the slates of its roof. Ravens plunged and swooped around it.

The wind whistled, flapping the blanket at Omnia's shoulders.

'Hello?' called Omnia.

There was no reply.

She made her way around the walkway to see if someone was waiting further around the turret.

No one. The walkway led her back towards the door to the Tower.

Then she saw him.

He stood at the door, wearing a long, black messenger's cloak, with a deep hood that dropped forward and threw his whole face into shadow.

Omnia stopped. Suddenly her mouth was dry. 'Are you the one who asked me to come here?' she said. She waited a moment. 'Did you leave the message for me?'

The figure didn't reply.

'What did you want to tell me?' demanded Omnia more loudly. 'Say it! I'm here.'

The other person took a step towards her. From under the hood came a low hissing.

'Who are you? Cornelius Slinker? Is that you? Show your face!'

The person lunged. Omnia jumped back and turned and tried to run. But already a hand was on her shoulder.

She screamed. Now the man's other hand caught her up and lifted her off her feet. Suddenly Omnia was in the air facing down with nothing but the blanket of mist below her. She reached back and clutched, desperately, grabbing for something, anything to hold on to. She had a handful of cloth, her attacker's cloak, perhaps, or hood. But it wasn't enough.

He hurled her off the Tower. She was falling.

11

An Unexpected Landing

She screamed. The cloak that she had clutched came with her and for an instant Omnia saw it fluttering above her like a black bird. Then somehow she had stopped her and she was bobbing up and down in mid-air, arms and legs entangled.

Then she was inside, in a room, sprawled on the floor.

A woman stood over her, holding a net.

'Who are you?' demanded the woman.

Omnia's heart was still pounding with the terror of the fall. What had just happened? Had that woman just caught her? In that net?

'Your name? Do you have a name?'

'Omnia Halibut,' murmured Omnia, staring at her.

The woman narrowed her eyes. They were so dark they were almost black. She seemed to be not much older than Omnia's own mother. Her hair, which was dark with strands of grey, was twisted in a plait that ran halfway down her back, and she had a strong face, with regular, harmonious features and lustrous skin.

'Never heard of you,' she said. 'Who are your parents?'

'My father's Evernear K Halibut and—'

'Evernear? Didn't he marry Candelia?'

'That's right,' said Omnia.

'So you're Evernear's daughter, are you? How old?'

'Twelve and a quarter.'

'Any brothers or sisters?'

'One brother.'

'Name?'

'Eversmooth T Halibut.'

'Age?'

'Seventeen and five-eighths.'

The woman nodded, frowning slightly in concentration as if filing the information away somewhere in her brain.

She sat down on a chair covered in red velvet, of which there were a number in the room, taking her net with her. The floor was made of grey slate and the walls of big blocks of grey stone, mostly covered with old, faded tapestries.

'Take a seat,' she said. She waved her hand around the room. 'Anywhere you like.'

Omnia got up and sat on one of the chairs, still trying to understand exactly how she had ended up inside this room.

The woman gazed at Omnia for so long that Omnia felt as if she was some kind of specimen under examination, and that the woman could somehow see under her skin.

'Who are you?' said Omnia.

'Basilica Halibut,' replied the woman.

'I've never heard of you.'

The woman laughed. 'I'd have fallen off my chair in surprise if you had.'

'Why?'

Basilica didn't answer. She simply raised an eyebrow.

'Did you catch me in that net?'

'So it seems.'

'What were you doing with it?'

'Saving you, I believe.'

'But why?'

'I would have thought you could answer that better than me.'

'No,' said Omnia. 'I mean, why did you have it? Why were you ready like that when I fell?'

'I go fishing sometimes.'

'Fishing?'

'Net-fishing, obviously. Not line-fishing. Early in the morning. Best time for it, ask any fisherperson.'

Omnia gazed at the woman uncomprehendingly.

'Fishing? Never heard of fishing?'

'But . . .'

'In the air, of course,' said Basilica impatiently. 'Can't do any other fishing from here, can you?'

'What do you catch?'

'Birds, mostly.'

'Then it's not fishing,' objected Omnia.

'Is it not? And I suppose you're the House fishing expert,

are you? I rather think that's Eversnare A Halibut. I rather think there's a thing or two he could teach even you on the subject.'

'He's dead.' Omnia looked at the woman incredulously. 'He's been dead for two years.'

'Oh.' Basilica frowned for a moment. 'Well, anyway, I dare say I know a thing or two more about fishing than you! If someone goes fishing in a lake and they pull up a boot, they've still gone fishing, haven't they? What do you think they've gone? Booting? And if they can pull in a boot, I don't see why I shouldn't be able to pull in a bird.'

'But they didn't intend to pull in a boot,' said Omnia.

'Nor I a bird!'

'But at least they had a *chance* of catching a fish!'

'Like me,' said Basilica.

'In the air?'

'You can catch all kinds of things in the air.'

'Like what?' demanded Omnia.

'Like a girl,' replied Basilica.

Omnia opened her mouth to reply – then she laughed.

'See?' said Basilica. 'Out I put my net and two seconds later, in you fall. I'd call it unexpected, at the least. In your place, I'd call it lucky.'

'I'd call it freakish.'

'If you like.'

Omnia frowned. 'I don't understand. If you want to go fishing, why don't you go *fishing*? Properly. It's not that I'm not grateful to you for catching me. But go to the Deep

Lake. Go to one of the streams. There are plenty of places to choose from.'

'Certainly, for those who can,' said Basilica.

'Why can't you? Don't you know where they are?' Omnia found it hard to believe that someone of Basilica's age wouldn't know where the lakes and streams were within the estate.

'Oh, I know where they are.'

Omnia stared at the woman in incomprehension. 'Then why don't you—'

'Tell me how you came to end up in my net.'

'But I still don't understand why you don't just—'

'I must say, I would have been happy with a raven this morning. Or a parrot. Or a pigeon, if it comes to that. Ever caught a pigeon? No, I wouldn't have thought so. There's a trick to it, you know. Don't imagine it's so simple. That's a common mistake. It's all in the way you use the net. Pigeons are slippery beasts, and if you don't do it properly, they'll escape every time. But . . .' Basilica raised a finger meaningfully. 'To return to the point. What were you doing falling outside my window this morning?'

Omnia hesitated. 'It's quite an extraordinary story.'

'So it should be,' remarked Basilica, 'to justify that kind of behaviour.'

'And as far as I can tell, completely without logic.'

'Nothing anyone does is without logic,' said the woman severely. 'Identify the motive and the logic will take care of itself.'

'Listen to this then,' said Omnia. She proceeded to tell the story, starting from the day she had seen someone coming out of the Wood at dawn, which was necessary in order to explain how she had discovered the hole in the wall, which was necessary in order to explain how she had found the message about the accident in the Hall of Leaning, which was necessary, at last, in order to explain how she had come to be falling from the top of the Slate Tower at six o'clock that morning.

But Basilica started laughing before she was even halfway through the story.

'What?' demanded Omnia.

'You put leaves at the bottom of the bar to see if it was moved? Whose idea was that?'

'Mine.' Omnia smiled ruefully. 'I suppose it wasn't very smart.'

'On the contrary, it was very smart. Or moderately smart at least. Your plan did have a flaw, of course. You didn't think anyone would check the bar before they removed it, did you?'

Omnia shook her head. It had never occurred to her.

'That should teach you. You're not up against fools. You'll have to do better next time.'

'What next time?'

'There'll be a next time, don't you worry.'

Omnia frowned. Basilica had said it in a tone of absolute certainty.

'It's not your plan that surprises me, it's the fact that

108

you did it. First, you had the curiosity to investigate the wall. Second, you had the originality to think of something like that. Not a perfect plan, but not a bad one. Third, you had the initiative to do it.' Basilica peered at her. 'Curiosity, originality, initiative. Are you sure you're a Halibut?'

'Of course I'm a Halibut!'

Basilica laughed again. 'What are the chances? Whoever it was coming out of the Wood knew they might be seen. It was a risk. Why do you think they'd take it? Because if they were seen, the chance of anyone in this Halibutarium actually bothering themselves to do anything about it would be ... well, I would have said zero. And yet he happens to be seen by the one person, apparently, who actually would. He must have got the shock of his life.' Basilica laughed. 'What *are* the chances?'

If you looked at it that way, thought Omnia, it was quite amusing. Or ironic, at least. And yet if you did look at it that way, it didn't say much for what Basilica thought of the rest of the Halibuts.

'You remind me of someone,' said Basilica.

'Who?'

'Doesn't matter. It was a long time ago.' Basilica sighed. 'That person no longer exists.'

'Was she a friend of yours?'

Basilica didn't reply to that. 'Let me ask you a question. Does the name make the person or does the person make the name?'

'Someone else asked me that,' said Omnia. 'Allevia Halibut. You know who she is, don't you?'

'I certainly do.'

'She asked me at the funeral feast.'

'Did she really? And what did you say?'

'I said it sounded like a riddle, and she said maybe it was my destiny to solve it. But I don't believe in destiny. I believe you make your own choices in life.'

'And what choices have you made, Omnia?' asked Basilica seriously.

'I made the choice to put the leaves in, for example.'

'Indeed you did.'

'And if I hadn't, I wouldn't be here today.'

Basilica nodded. She gazed silently at Omnia.

'Shall I finish the story?'

'Yes,' said Basilica. 'Tell me the rest.'

Omnia finished telling her how she had come to be falling past her window so early in the morning. 'What I can't work out,' she said, 'is whether the person up there had really come to throw me off the Tower or whether he had actually come to tell me something and somehow there was some kind of misunderstanding and it ended up like that. It didn't seem like it, but then I don't know why anyone would want to do that to me.' Omnia paused. 'He couldn't have thought I was attacking him, could he?'

'Do you have any idea who it was?' asked Basilica.

Omnia didn't reply. It could have been Cornelius Slinker. He was about Slinker's height, and that was all she had to go on. The irony of it was that as she reached back and pulled the cloak loose, she had been facing the other way and hadn't been able to get a look at his face.

Basilica raised an eyebrow.

'I have a suspicion,' said Omnia.

Basilica waited, but Omnia didn't speak.

'Quite right, Omnia. Never jump to conclusions.'

'But I still can't work out whether he was trying to—'

'Oh, there's no doubt about that,' interjected Basilica. 'Let's not fool ourselves. He was trying to kill you, my dear.'

Omnia stared.

'And he was trying to kill you when the tile fell in the Hall of Leaning. That was no accident. He dropped it on you. It was the same person, of course. But I assume you'd worked that out for yourself.'

'You say that very calmly,' said Omnia.

'What do I have to be alarmed about? It's you he's trying to kill, Omnia, not me. I'm perfectly safe.'

Omnia nodded. Basilica had a point.

'And the message written in the ground. What do you think you'd find if you went back there now?'

Omnia had no intention of going back there. The thought made her shiver.

'Nothing. I'd bet you anything you like those words have been rubbed out. No evidence that anyone ever told you to go to the Tower. Just a note saying "Look to the left", isn't that what you said? What does that mean? Nothing.

Imagine if you'd been found at the bottom of the Tower. What would people have thought?'

Omnia thought about it. 'An accident,' she murmured.

'Exactly. An accident. Even if they'd found that note on your body it wouldn't have meant a thing. Now let's think about the situation. Someone's trying to kill you, and trying to make it look like an accident. We don't know who – although you obviously have a suspicion – and we don't know why, although we suspect it's got something to do with the fact that you found a hole in the wall which that person may very well be using.'

'But the leaves weren't disturbed,' pointed out Omnia.

'Yes, but if *you* could place them round the bar, so could someone else after he went in or out. Or perhaps he decided not to use the hole until he had got rid of you. Now, this person may suspect that you know who he is, and even if he doesn't, he may think you'll reveal that the hole is being used. That in itself might be enough to spoil his plans. So he decides to kill you.' Basilica paused. 'He has a motive, doesn't he? Are you still going to tell me there's no logic in the story?'

There was, thought Omnia.

'By the way, I think we should also assume this person knows you're not dead. If you've just hurled someone off a tower, the first thing you'd do is look over the edge.'

'So he would have seen you save me!'

'Probably. Even as we speak, he's probably trying to find a way in here.'

Omnia looked around in alarm.

Basilica smiled. 'There's a reason I have to do my fishing in the air.'

'What is that? Why *do*—'

'Omnia, there's only one question that's really important at the moment. He's tried to kill you once. He's tried to kill you twice. The question is—'

'Will he try to kill me a third time?'

'I think the answer to that is fairly obvious. The real question is: what will he do if you don't give him a third chance?'

'Why should he do anything?'

'Omnia, this person, whoever it is, he's not trying to kill you because he doesn't like you. He's killing you because you know something – that he's coming and going through that hole in the wall. That's a threat to him. What's he coming and going for? There must be a purpose and it must be a secret. What will he do now if he can't get to you and he thinks he's about to be discovered?'

'Wait a second! How do you know he's using the hole to come in and out?'

'What other explanation is there?'

Omnia frowned. She had never heard of anything like this happening before. It *had* occurred to her that someone might be using the hole in the wall, of course. That was why she had left the leaves. But if they were using it, it would have been an extraordinary thing. Not the kind of thing you just casually imagine happening.

'I don't understand this!' said Omnia at last. 'You talk as if it's the most normal thing in the world, as if you've seen it all before.'

'Do I?'

'Yes! And it isn't normal. It isn't normal to have someone going in and out through a hole in the wall, is it? And I don't think it's normal to have someone dropping a tile on me in the Hall of Leaning. Or on anyone, actually. And I absolutely don't think it's normal for someone to throw me off the top of the Slate Tower. And I had to get up early for that!'

'Just think, if it was later, I mightn't have caught you.'

'Well, even so! It isn't normal! It absolutely isn't normal!'

'I agree,' said Basilica. 'On the other hand, it isn't abnormal.' She paused. 'Listen to me, Omnia. There are things that have happened in Neversuch House.'

'Like what? Things like this? I've never heard of them!'

'There are things no one speaks of. There are people no one mentions.'

'Who?'

Basilica gazed at her. Then she said: 'You mentioned a funeral feast. You mentioned Allevia Halibut. Everwise is dead, isn't he?'

Omnia nodded.

'When did he die?'

'A few days ago.' Omnia paused. 'Are you saying you don't know?'

'What was the cause?'

Omnia stared. 'You *don't* know, do you? You didn't even know he was dead. How can you not know something like that?'

'How did he die?'

'He fell down the stairs from the Hall of Puppets.'

'Really? It was an accident, I suppose?'

Omnia nodded.

'Did anyone see it happen?'

'No.' Omnia frowned. 'Are you saying it wasn't an accident? Are you saying this has got something to do with it?'

'How would I know, Omnia? I wasn't there.'

'But from the way you said—'

'Who's the new Captain?'

'Everdean.'

'Everdean P Halibut? But he was older than Everwise. Surely Everwise didn't nominate Everdean!'

'Everwise didn't nominate anybody. Allevia told me that was the greatest joke he played.'

Basilica shook her head. 'That would be just like him. A spiteful man, at least in his later years. I should know better than most. That man loved his puppets more than he ever loved any living person.'

'Well, it's a terrible thing to do, not telling us who the next Captain should be. And no one seems to be willing to do anything about it. They all laugh at Everdean, but no one says they're prepared to do the job.'

'Nothing changes,' murmured Basilica to herself. She frowned. 'So Everdean's the Captain, is he?'

115

'Temporarily. No one knows how the permanent Captain is going to be chosen.'

'Omnia, you've only got one chance to find the person who tried to kill you.'

'But you just said he'll try again!'

'Exactly. So you must trap him.'

'Shouldn't I *tell* someone about this? The Butler or someone?'

'You can.'

Omnia watched her. The way Basilica had said 'can', it obviously didn't mean 'should'.

'I doubt they'd believe you,' said Basilica.

'I could tell them about you. I could tell them you caught me.'

'No! That's the worst thing you could do.' Basilica gazed at her severely. 'Don't you dare tell anyone you've seen me. Promise.'

'Why?'

'Because it won't do either of us any good. Believe me. I know what I'm saying.'

'Why not? You could tell them you caught me.'

Basilica shook her head.

'You wouldn't?'

'Listen to me, Omnia. There's very little I can do for you, but I can tell you this. If you want to survive, rely on yourself, no one else. You must force this person into the open. Before you tell anyone anything, if you want to be believed, you must force him to show himself. That's how

116

you'll be safe.' Basilica paused. 'The question is how. You could go back to the hole in the wall and wait for him there.'

'I'm not going anywhere near it! That's exactly what he'd expect. He'd trap *me*.'

Basilica smiled. 'Very good. Exactly. Send someone else.'

'No! Then *they*'d get killed.'

'Right again.'

'Then what should I do?'

'That, I don't know. But here's what I think. If he knows you're alive, and he can't find you, then whatever he's planning to do – whatever his real motive is – he'll do it quickly, before he can be found out. He'll make a move, possibly one he doesn't want to make. He might be forced to take a risk.'

'What will it be?'

'I have no idea. But if you're lucky, he'll reveal himself by what he does. Your best way to force him into the open is to stay safe until it happens.'

'He probably knows I live in the Long South Range.'

'I'd assume that, if I were you.'

'Where can I hide?'

Basilica didn't reply immediately. She was silent, as if weighing up something in her mind. 'Do you know the Ribbled Lodge?' she asked eventually.

Omnia nodded.

'Do you know how to get there?'

'Yes.'

Basilica beckoned to her, and Omnia got up and sat on the chair beside her. Quietly, almost in a whisper, Basilica told her where to go when she got to the Ribbled Lodge. Omnia listened with concentration.

'And don't let anyone else know where you are,' said Basilica. 'Promise.'

Omnia nodded. 'All right. How do I find you if I need you?'

'Omnia, I don't know what else I could possibly do for you.'

'But how do I find you?'

'I'm always here.'

'But how do I get to you?'

'I fish.'

Omnia stared at her doubtfully. 'There must be another—'

'Below the door at the top of the tower.'

'You're not seriously saying—'

'Every fisherperson has a spot. That's mine.'

Omnia looked at the woman doubtfully. 'But wouldn't you at least need to know I'm coming? Don't you need some warning?'

'Early in the morning is good,' said Basilica. 'The fish are always biting.'

Omnia watched her, still trying to see if she was serious.

Basilica got up. She pulled aside a tapestry. Behind it was a small, square door in the wall. She opened it, revealing the entrance to a narrow chute.

'You remember where I told you to go? You remember how to find it?'

Omnia nodded.

'Go straight there. That's where you should wait. As long as no one sees you, you'll be safe.'

Omnia crouched to get into the chute.

'Feet first,' said Basilica.

But Omnia straightened up again. 'I'm still not sure I shouldn't tell anyone. I'm not sure I shouldn't tell the Butler.'

'Tell him – if you don't value your life.'

'How do I know that's true?'

'I can only give you my advice. You promised not to mention me. As long as you don't do that, Omnia, it's up to you. You can take my advice or leave it.'

'How do I know you're not part of this? You caught me in a net. What are the chances of that happening?'

'Extremely low, I would have thought. On the other hand, if I was trying to kill you, I wouldn't have caught you at all.'

'Maybe you're not trying to kill me. Maybe you're trying to do something else. You just told me to hide in the Ribbled Lodge. Maybe you and this other person are just trying to get me there for some reason. He drops me, you catch me, and I run off to where you both want me.'

'That's possible,' said Basilica. 'In fact, it would be quite an elegant plot. The only problem is, Omnia, I lack a motive. Still, perhaps you can think of one.' Basilica paused. 'No? Shame. I'd have been interested to hear what you thought it was. Doesn't mean I don't have one, of course. Still, if that's the plan, surely you don't expect me to admit it.'

'So you don't deny it?'

'I don't deny it's possible. I deny it's true. But then I also don't deny that if I was in your shoes, I might think that I was lying.' Basilica shrugged. 'You'll have to decide for yourself.'

Omnia looked at her uncertainly.

Basilica was still holding open the door of the chute. 'Feet first,' she said crisply.

12

Night

Omnia gripped a branch and hoisted herself up. The ivy was a huge, ancient plant, densely covering the wall. Its main trunk was as thick as an oak, and in the days of Evergreen Halibut, a tree house had been constructed to hang from its branches. The tree house was long gone, yet the ivy still grew against the wall like a young vine, and every spring the gardeners had to slash it back from the windows to prevent it growing over the sills and sealing them forever.

But the wall against which it grew wasn't the wall of the Ribbled Lodge, where Basilica had told Omnia to go.

Darkness had fallen and Omnia was deep in the shadows of the ivy as she climbed. She felt for the branches, one after the other. The leaves brushed at her face. She kept climbing until she was three storeys up. At last, she stopped and tapped on a window. She waited, hanging on to the ivy.

She tapped again, louder. Then she rapped on the glass as hard as she dared. The window opened. A head looked out.

'Evergrow,' whispered Omnia. 'Over here.'

Her cousin looked around and almost fell back at the sight of her. 'Omnia! What are you doing there?'

'*Shhhhhh!* I just thought I'd hang around in the ivy for a while. And then I thought, why not drop by and visit Evergrow?'

'Really?'

'No. Let me in!'

Evergrow stepped back and Omnia climbed inside. She quickly drew the curtain.

Evergrow watched her suspiciously. 'What's going on? Where were you today? I tried to find you and no one knew where you were.'

'Why were you trying to find me?' demanded Omnia.

'No reason,' said Evergrow. 'I just . . . what's going on?'

'Is your door locked?'

Evergrew shook his head.

'Go and lock it.'

Evergrow went to the door. Omnia sat down on the floor, right there under the window. She let her head rest against the wall. She was tired and hungry.

Evergrow came back to her. 'Where were you today?'

'It doesn't matter. Have you got any food?'

'Not much. I can go and—'

'No! Have you got anything here?'

'Let me see.' Evergrow went to a chest of drawers. He began looking through one of them, pulling out pine cones and bits of wood and chunks of rock.

Omnia watched him, hoping he would find something to eat amongst the collection of objects he was pulling out. She was too hungry to care what it was. She hadn't eaten all day.

The chute out of Basilica Halibut's room had taken her down a fast, spiralling ride and dumped her in a tunnel. She followed it until she came to a series of large grilles in the floor. Creeping silently across them, Omnia had found herself looking down on a roomful of cooks hacking and cutting at wooden chopping boards, surrounded by carcases and meats of all kinds. She saw barrels of fish in ice and bunches of game birds tied by their feet and fat-streaked carcases of pigs and skinned deer and huge sides of beef hanging off hooks directly below her. She realised that the tunnel must have brought her under the Great Kitchen Court and she was looking down on the butchery that served the kitchens. But there was no way out of the tunnel here and she moved on. The tunnel grew very dark and Omnia had to feel her way until light showed up ahead. Here she found a set of stairs that led to a small, arched opening, barely more than half a metre in height. She crept up to it and peered out cautiously. In front of her, across an expanse of stone, was the Purple Nave.

And that was where she had waited, all day, head down, until night fell to cloak the House in darkness, when finally she had stretched herself flat under the opening and crawled out.

Evergrow came back from the drawers with a handful of sweets. Bits of lint and fragments of rock stuck to them, but Omnia was ready to eat just about anything.

Evergrow looked in other drawers. He turned around with something else in his hand. 'Do you want this?'

'What is it?'

'I don't know. It looks like dried fruit or something.' Evergrow took a nibble and scrunched up his face, trying to work out what it was. 'I don't know. I really don't know what it is.' He took another nibble. 'Actually, it's not bad. I'll have it if you won't.'

'I'll have it,' said Omnia, and Evergrow reluctantly handed it over.

Omnia ate whatever it was that Evergrow had found. Then she went back to the sweets.

She looked around the room. On the floor beside a chest of drawers was a huge purple felt boot. Omnia gazed at it. 'Is that the boot you got from Everwise's rooms?'

Evergrow nodded.

Omnia smiled. Even after everything that had happened to her that day, the sight of that enormous boot was so ridiculous it made her want to laugh. 'Evergrow, it's so big, you could put both your feet into it and it'd still be too big!'

Evergrow shrugged.

'What are you going to do with it?'

Evergrow looked at the boot, frowning. 'I might grow into it.'

'If you become the biggest Halibut ever. And so what? You've only got one.'

'I can get another one made.'

'Like that one? A purple boot?'

Evergrow's frown grew deeper. He continued to stare at the boot. 'It was the only thing I could get. I don't know why I took it, really.' He was silent for a moment, as if trying to work it out. Then he shrugged and looked back at her. 'Are you going to tell me what's going on?'

Omnia nodded. She told him. Evergrow started to laugh when she told him about being caught in a net, but he stopped when he saw Omnia's reaction.

This wasn't a joke. Omnia knew she was in real danger. If that net hadn't suddenly poked out of the Slate Tower – whatever Basilica's real reason for doing it – she would have been dead.

'That really happened?' said Evergrow. 'She caught you?'

'Every word I've said is true. Only you can't tell anyone I saw her. I wasn't even meant to tell you.'

'Why not?'

'I don't know, but you mustn't mention her. Promise.'

Evergrow shrugged. 'All right.' He thought for a moment, then shook his head in amazement, thinking about what Omnia had told him. 'That's extraordinary, Omnia. That's an extraordinary event.'

No more extraordinary than being thrown off a tower by

a hooded man in the first place, thought Omnia. Which *was* an extraordinary event, now that she thought about it, if not a once-in-a-lifetime experience. Or an end-of-a-lifetime experience. They seemed to be coming thick and fast, these extraordinary events. Omnia had a feeling they weren't over yet.

She told him the rest, about her conversation with Basilica and her exit via the tunnel that ran across the kitchen butchery.

'So what's for lunch tomorrow?' asked Evergrow.

'Very funny.'

Evergrow's face became serious again. 'What are you going to do?'

'I'm going to wait,' replied Omnia. 'Basilica was right. I just happened to get in the way. I'm not what this is about.'

'What *is* it about?'

'That's what I need to find out. If I wait, maybe he'll do something that will show me.'

Evergrow picked up one of the sweets from the pile in front of Omnia, brushed the lint off it and put it in his mouth.

'Why didn't you go where Basilica sent you?' he asked.

Omnia shrugged.

'You don't trust her, do you?'

'She saved me, but it's suspicious,' said Omnia. 'Don't you think?'

'More than suspicious. Are you sure that really happened?'

'I *told* you.' Omnia frowned. 'If I went where she told me, I don't know who might be waiting for me when I got

126

there. I need someone I can trust.' She glanced at Evergrow. '*Really* trust.'

'Well, you came to the right person.'

Omnia knew that. She and Evergrow had been born only a couple of months apart and had always been close. They had grown up virtually side by side. Omnia didn't think her cousin was the bravest boy in the world, or the most imaginative, but if there was one thing she was sure of, he was reliable and trustworthy. He had never betrayed any of the secrets she had told him. When she was trying to think of somewhere she could go, someone she could trust to help hide her, Evergrow's name was the one she immediately thought of.

'I only wish Everlook was here,' said Evergrow. 'You could trust him too.'

Omnia nodded. Everlook J Halibut had been their uncle, the brother of Omnia's father, Evernear, and Evergrow's mother, Ribelia. He had been much younger than them, only ten years older than Omnia and Evergrow themselves, and when they were growing up, he had been more of a big brother than an uncle, always laughing and playing with them. And then a couple of years earlier, at the age of twenty, he had suddenly died, apparently having fallen from a stair that had crumbled in the High North Lodge. No one was even allowed to see his body, so mangled was it by the fall. One day he was here and the next he was gone and all that was left was a mound for him in the Field of Dreams, and he would never laugh and play with them again.

Omnia missed her uncle, but Evergrow had taken his

death even harder. Barely a day went by when he didn't mention him.

'I was hoping I could wait here,' said Omnia.

'Of course you can. Everlook would hide you, wouldn't he? I will too.'

Suddenly there was a banging on the door, followed by shouting and giggling.

'Go away!' yelled Evergrow.

The giggling and banging continued.

'Maybe not,' said Omnia. Evergrow's two younger brothers were terrible chatterboxes and gigglers, and now they were demanding to be let in.

'Go away!' yelled Evergrow again. 'Don't worry,' he whispered to Omnia, 'if you ignore them long enough, they'll get tired of it.'

'Maybe I should go.'

'No, you can stay here. This is the safest place.' He turned to the door. 'Go *away!*'

There was silence for a moment, then the giggling and banging started up again.

Evergrow shrugged. 'You can hide in the wardrobe. It's huge. When I was little, I used to pretend it went on and on, I didn't know where to, and anything could come out of it, even monsters. Remember?'

Omnia smiled. 'You used to scare yourself so much you couldn't get to sleep.'

'You can do things like that when you're little,' said Evergrow nostalgically.

Omnia sighed. That was true.

'We'll make a bed for you in there.'

'Thanks, Evergrow. I won't be any trouble. Just bring me some food. And the news.'

Evergrow was silent for a moment. 'Shouldn't we tell someone about this? Digby or someone? It must be safe to tell the Butler.'

It was the question Omnia had asked Basilica herself. She shook her head. 'Once I'm out, whoever it is who's doing this will come after me again. Basilica said he would and I think she's right.'

'And you have no idea who it was?'

'I couldn't see his face, I told you.'

'But you must have some idea.'

Omnia hesitated. 'I'm not sure. If I tell you, it's a secret. You can't tell anyone else.'

Evergrow nodded.

She hesitated a moment longer. 'I think it may be Cornelius Slinker.'

Evergrow's eyes narrowed thoughtfully. 'I've always thought he looked suspicious. He's always creeping around. And he never says anything. He just stares at you.'

'I've got no proof though. I'm sure Basilica's right, I'm sure the words in the ground will be gone by now. So even if I do tell the Butler, what's he going to do? Why should he believe me?'

'He can ask Basilica.'

'She doesn't know who it is.'

'But she caught you, isn't that what you said? She can tell him that, at least. That'll prove you're not making this up. You must have been thrown off the Tower – you wouldn't just jump, would you, and hope someone catches you?'

Omnia shook her head. 'I can't do that.'

'What?'

'I can't mention her. I told you. She told me I mustn't.'

'But what if you do?'

'She told me not to. She said it would be the worst thing I could do for both of us. The way she said it, Evergrow, I think she really meant it.'

'Do you?' said Evergrow doubtfully. 'Do you really trust her?'

'I don't know if I trust her or not. But if we tell Digby, I have no proof and she told me not to mention her. If I do, she might deny ever having seen me, and where does that leave me? Looking more like a liar than ever! And in the mean time, *he'll* be out there, waiting for his chance to get me again.'

Omnia had spent the whole day thinking about this, waiting for nightfall to come so she could leave the tunnel under the Purple Nave. She didn't know what she trusted of what Basilica had said and what she didn't. But there were two things she did know. If Basilica denied having caught her, she would have no proof at all to make anyone else believe her story. And in the mean time, the killer would be looking for her. Those two things meant she had only one option.

130

'Evergrow, all I can do right now is make sure he doesn't have that chance. If he can't find me, he'll do something else. With any luck, if it is Cornelius, that's how he'll show himself. So that's what I'm going to do – unless you've got a better idea.'

'No,' murmured Evergrow. He was silent, thinking. At last, he nodded. 'All right. No one saw you climbing up here, did they?'

'I don't think so.'

'Then you're safe.' Evergrow went to the window and pulled the curtain back slightly. He peered out into the darkness.

'Omnia,' he said.

'What?'

'Come here.'

'Someone will see me.'

'Come here!' Evergrow's voice was urgent.

Omnia turned off the light and went to the window. Evergrow pointed up through the gap in the curtains.

High in the sky, in the light of the moon, flew a great black bird. It was just as everyone had been saying, enormous, the size of a person.

Omnia watched as the bird circled above the House. Then it wheeled in the air, and for an instant Omnia felt as if she and the bird were gazing directly into each other's eyes, although Omnia couldn't make out the creature's face and it couldn't possibly have seen her behind the window in the darkened room. Yet for some reason, as

131

the bird turned in the moonlight, it seemed to Omnia as if it was there only for her, as if they were exchanging not glances, but thoughts.

The bird dipped its wing, swung away, and disappeared into the night.

13

Behind the Ivy

The wardrobe was deep. It was more like a dark, blind-ended corridor. There were a huge number of jumpers, scarves, hats and gloves stacked on shelves. Evergrow's mother, Ribelia, was always knitting and Evergrow got something new at least once a week, although he hardly ever wore any of it. The clothes that he actually used were scattered all over the floor. Far inside the wardrobe, against the back wall, they made a bed for Omnia out of blankets and pillows.

It took a long time for her to fall asleep. She kept thinking of the moment she fell from the Tower. It was sheer terror, the feeling of falling, falling, falling into nothingness. And had she glimpsed a face looking down at her from the top of the Tower? Above the fluttering black cloak? Was there an instant when the edge of the cloak had fluttered back and she had seen a face?

Omnia tried to remember, concentrating as hard as she

could. *Was* it Cornelius Slinker? She had a feeling that she might have seen a face, but try as she would, she couldn't capture the exact moment. If she had seen who it was, the features escaped her. Perhaps the terror of falling had driven them out of her mind. The terror came back to her. And then suddenly, inexplicably, she had been bouncing up and down in Basilica's net.

As for Basilica, it seemed that every answer she had given to Omnia's questions opened up another five. Everyone said the falling tile in the Hall of Leaning was an accident – Basilica had said that someone had been aiming for her as if it was the most obvious thing in the world. Omnia had the feeling that Basilica doubted whether Everwise's death was an accident as well.

Why would it be the worst thing she could do to tell anyone she had seen her? Not just for Basilica, or for Omnia, but for both of them, if you could believe what Basilica said. And what was she doing there anyway, all alone in the Slate Tower where no one lived, apparently unable to leave, 'fishing' with a net in the air? Where was the door to her room? Omnia realised that all the way up the staircase she hadn't seen a single door. She didn't know what was the more extraordinary of the events that had happened to her that day, having someone try to kill her at the top of the Slate Tower or being saved by Basilica Halibut halfway down.

So many questions. Eventually Omnia fell asleep pondering them, and when she awoke, Evergrow was gone.

He was soon back with pockets full of jam rolls and apple pastries and a pair of peaches in his hands. He made sure it was safe for Omnia to use the bathroom, which was two doors down the corridor, and he made sure it was safe for her to slip back into his room. Then he went out again. He would be much more use outside, Omnia knew, where he would hear about anything that happened, than keeping her company in his room.

Yet it was boring in there all by herself. She stayed inside the wardrobe most of the time, in case someone came into the room unexpectedly. She sat near the back, legs crossed, elbows on her knees, thinking. Someone was out to kill her, was probably looking for her right now. The idea sent shivers down her spine. What was going to happen? Something would happen – it had to. She thought about it, tapping her fingers absently along the back wall.

She stopped. She tapped again. A hollow sound. She looked around. The wall behind her was blank, painted a light colour. She had once seen one of the Gondoliers tapping along a wall in her father's library to find the spot where he knew there had once been a door into the adjacent room, which Omnia's father wanted to have opened again. A hollow sound meant there was hardly anything between one room and the next, the mason had explained to her. A thin sheet of wood, perhaps, or plaster. A dull sound meant there was solid brick.

Omnia tapped along the wall at intervals just as she had

seen the mason do it. *Dull, hollow, hollow, hollow, hollow, hollow, dull.* She did it again. *Dull, hollow, hollow, hollow, hollow, hollow, dull.* She could tap out a gap in the brick. It was the width of a narrow door.

After the mason had tapped out an area in the wall of her father's library, he had picked up a hammer and smashed it through. He had even let her strike a couple of blows. The plaster had disintegrated with surprising ease.

Omnia tapped again along the bottom of the wall, just to be sure.

It wasn't her wall. It wasn't her wardrobe. And if Omnia Halibut had been a more cautious person, like her cousin Evergrow, for example, she would have left it at that. But if Omnia Halibut had been a more cautious person, she wouldn't have been thrown off the Slate Tower and ended up hiding in her cousin's wardrobe in the first place.

She stood up, put her arm against the wall to steady herself, balanced on one leg, and smashed the bottom of the wall with her heel.

Her foot went straight through.

Omnia quickly got down on her knees and put her hand through the hole. There was some kind of space on the other side because even with her arm all the way in, she couldn't feel anything. She tore pieces of plaster away. Soon she had opened a hole big enough to crawl through. She put her head through the hole. Dark. She went in.

The air on the other side was close and stale. The light was very dim. It took a while for her eyes to adjust.

It seemed to be a kind of long, narrow room. There were things in here. She made out a chair. A table. And there were windows on one side, but only a few weak rays of light filtered through.

She went to a window. Black leaves were squashed against the glass outside. The ivy.

But the gardeners cut back the vine every spring to make sure the windows would remain unblocked. And yet these ones had been left. Once they had been left for a few years, Omnia imagined, the gardeners wouldn't even know they were supposed to cut here. From outside, she guessed, there was no sign of this window at all.

Omnia ran a finger over the windowsill. Dust. Deep dust.

'Evergrow?'

Omnia froze. She recognised the voice. It was Evergrow's mother, Ribelia.

'Evergrow?'

Omnia looked back at the wall through which she had come. On this side, there was a pointed wooden archway which must have once been the entrance, blocked off by plaster. At the bottom was the ragged hole she had made when breaking through.

Omnia heard footsteps coming closer.

'Evergrow D Halibut . . .' Ribelia's voice was coming from just the other side of the wall now as she murmured to herself. '*Why don't you ever wear anything I make you?*' There was a sigh. '*Well, maybe you'll wear this.*'

Omnia smiled. Ribelia had obviously knitted *another* thing for Evergrow. She just didn't get the message.

But the smile didn't last for long. Omnia could hear the rustle of clothes. *'Always throwing things on the floor.'* Ribelia was clearing up! She only had to look around in the dimness of the wardrobe to see the blankets and pillows where Omnia had slept and to see the hole she had made in the wall.

The muttering and rustling went on. Would Ribelia look? Omnia could hardly stand the tension. Suddenly she was certain she was going to sneeze. There was so much dust in here, surely she would. Her nose started to prickle.

'Such a messy boy!'

Omnia squeezed her nose, trying to hold on.

Suddenly she heard one of Evergrow's brothers.

'Not now,' said Ribelia.

The boy whined.

'I said not— Stop pulling me. Stop! Stop! Oh, you're so naughty. All right then. Where are you taking me?'

The boy laughed. There were footsteps and then the sound of a door closing.

Silence.

Omnia waited. Still silence.

It was the first time Omnia had ever been grateful for one of Evergrow's brothers, who were such whiny, noisy, annoying little boys.

She went back to the hole and got down on her hands and knees and peered into the wardrobe. It was empty.

She reached through and pulled back a couple of pillows to cover up the hole from the other side. Then she backed away and stood up again.

Omnia's eyes had entirely adjusted to the dimness of the light now and she was able to make out what was in the room. Near one of the windows stood an armchair thickly draped with cobwebs. On the opposite side of the room the walls were covered with wood panelling. Two paintings hung there. Omnia went closer. One of the paintings was of the face of a beautiful young woman.

Omnia gazed at it. The face reminded her of Basilica. Something about the shape of the face and the eyes. *Could it be Basilica? Surely not. How could it be?* But there was something about the painting that did make Omnia think of her. How old was the woman in the painting? Young, very young. If it was Basilica, Omnia thought, it would have to have been painted years before. She tried to work out how long. If Basilica was as old as her own mother, it must be twenty years at least. Maybe even thirty.

She looked at the second painting. It showed the same young woman and a man, who looked quite young as well, standing together. She didn't recognise the man. They were shown outside, smiling, and the skyline of the House was behind them. Omnia could make out the Great Tower and the Slate Tower far to its right.

Under the painting stood a large chest of drawers. Omnia tried one of the drawers. It didn't open.

She turned around. A wooden table stood against the

wall between two of the windows on the other side of the room, with a single chair drawn up to it. On the table was a candlestick with wax hanging like frozen water-falls from its two holders. There was a single plate and cutlery, a wine glass, a jug and a birdcage on one corner of the table. Omnia tried to imagine this room with the ivy cut back from the windows and light streaming in and a bird – a small green parrot, perhaps – chirping in the cage.

The dust on the table was so thick it had almost formed into a crust. There was nothing in the glass, only a faint dark staining at the bottom. The plate was bare as well. Omnia picked it up and blew the dust off. As she did, she noticed something at the bottom of the birdcage. She peered closer. It was the skeleton of a small bird. Why would anyone leave a bird in its cage after it had died to rot away to a skeleton?

Omnia looked back at the plate. There was a kind of black crust on one part of it, nothing else. Omnia scraped at it and a little of the crust came off under her fingernail. She put the plate back. The knife and fork weren't set out on either side of it, but lying at angles, as if carelessly flung down, as if someone had been eating a meal and had been interrupted. But where was the food? Gone, rotted away, or mice could have got to it and only the black crust was left.

Strange. How long was it since anyone else had been here, since the room had been sealed and the ivy had been allowed to grow over its windows, concealing its existence?

It must have happened at least before Evergrow and his family had moved into the apartment outside, and maybe much longer ago than that.

Suddenly Omnia realised that she was the first person who had stood inside this room for years, for decades. She looked at the painting of the young woman again. Basilica? She wiped the dust off it. Even in the dimness of the light, the face was as fresh as if only a day or a week had passed since the moment it was completed.

In this silent, sealed chamber, since the day the door had been closed off, time had stood still.

But outside, time isn't standing still. It never does. As Omnia looks around the room behind the ivy with its thick layers of dust, events in Neversuch House are moving on.

14

The Bass Bell

Evergrow heard the rumour from the twins. He bumped into them in the square in front of the Unicorn House, which was named for the horned statue of a rearing unicorn that stood high up at each corner of its roof. The twins bobbed around excitedly in front of him, wearing purple sunhats, dying to tell him the news, yet somehow so excited that they couldn't quite get to the point.

'I don't believe it for a second,' said Artesia.

'I do,' snapped Evesia.

'What?' asked Evergrow.

'She'd never do it! Never!' said Artesia.

'Of course she would!' snapped Evesia.

'What?' demanded Evergrow.

'It's not like her.'

'It's exactly like her!'

'*What?*' cried Evergrow.

The two girls looked at him.

'Omnia was seen outside the wall,' said Evesia.

'Outside the wall?' asked Evergrow incredulously.

Evesia nodded self-righteously. 'Outside the wall. In the city.'

'I don't believe it!' cried Artesia. 'It's a lie!'

'When?' said Evergrow.

'Yesterday.'

'Yesterday?' murmured Evergrow.

'It's not true!'

'Of course it's true,' said Evesia. 'Where was she yesterday? Where? Did you see her?'

Artesia refused to answer.

'Evergrow? Did you?'

He shook his head.

'See!'

'It can't be true,' insisted Artesia. 'How could she do it? Just walk out through the gate? They wouldn't let her out.'

'She'd find a way.'

'What way?'

'Another way. She'd find a way.'

'No, she wouldn't. She'd *never* do it. Right, Evergrow? She wouldn't, would she? No one would.'

Evergrow frowned. 'Umm . . . No. She wouldn't.'

'He doesn't sound very convinced,' murmured Evesia slyly, nudging her sister with her elbow.

'Of course he's convinced! He just said it, didn't he?'

'Who said they saw her?' asked Evergrow.

The two girls looked at each other and shrugged.

'Everyone's talking about it,' said Evesia. '*Everyone* knows.'

'Must have been a servant,' said Artesia.

'There!' cried Evesia. 'You see! You do believe it.'

'I don't! But it must be a servant who said it, mustn't it? It couldn't be a Halibut who claimed to have seen her because that would mean they'd been outside the wall as well.'

Evesia's eyes narrowed under her sunhat, as if she was trying to work out whether her sister was trying to trick her in some way. 'I suppose not,' she conceded eventually.

'Which servant?' asked Evergrow.

'Must be one who was outside the wall himself.' Evesia grinned maliciously. 'They'll *kill* her if they catch her.'

'They won't *kill* her,' retorted Artesia.

'Just about! What's the punishment for being outside the wall?'

The twins looked at Evergrow. He had no idea. He wasn't aware of anyone who had ever done it. He had always been told that no Halibut had ever been outside the wall simply because no true Halibut would ever want to. It was simply inconceivable that Omnia had chosen to do so.

'Maybe they won't let her back in,' said Evesia. 'That'd serve her right! She'll have to live out *there* and spend *every* day working just so she has enough to eat so she can get up and work again tomorrow.' Evesia giggled at the thought and danced a joyful little jig, her purple sunhat flapping at her ears. 'That's what I'd do to her.'

'That's because you're horrible!' cried Artesia.

'Don't blame me! I'm not the one who went outside the wall. And you'll never be able to be friends with her again, Artesia. Never ever ever. You'll be as bad as her if you are.'

'That's awful! Don't say that!'

'Never ever ever! Never ever ever!'

'That's . . . That's . . .' But Artesia couldn't get the words out, and her lip trembled, and suddenly she burst into tears and ran away.

Evesia looked at Evergrow, grinned and then ran after her sister, her purple sunhat flapping around her head.

Evergrow looked around the square in front of the Unicorn House. It was known as the Court of the Spouted Fountain because of a huge, ornate fountain at its centre, but the water in the fountain ran erratically, for reasons none of the plumbers could determine, and it had been dry for months. Around the square, people stood talking. Evergrow moved closer to one small group, pretending to be looking at something far off in the sky, and immediately heard Omnia's name being mentioned. It was the same when he walked past some other people. There was nothing Halibuts loved so much as a rumour. Everyone was talking about it.

Evergrow didn't know what to think. He sat down against the wall of the Unicorn House in a daze. Omnia? His very own cousin, his best friend? *Could* she have gone outside the wall?

It wasn't impossible. Where had she been the previous

day? No one had seen her. As for how she could have got out, Evergrow knew something no one else did. Omnia had a way, straight through the hole in the wall that she had discovered. Maybe she'd done it. Maybe she really had.

And then she had come back to him to hide her, producing the most ridiculous story he had ever heard. Being thrown off a tower, being caught in the air. By someone, conveniently, he wasn't allowed to mention.

That was what really hurt him, the fact that Omnia thought he'd believe a story like that. Just what kind of an idiot did she think he was?

And he *had* believed it. That was what hurt even more.

Well, if that was the kind of game she wanted to play, it would be easy enough to do something about it. All he had to do was go to the Butler and tell him where she was. He'd like to see what story she'd tell then!

But what would they do to her? What *was* the punishment for going over the wall? There had to be one, thought Evergrow, even if it had never been used. He was still in a kind of shock at the thought of Omnia doing something like that. He couldn't understand what had got into her. The punishment must be really horrible. Did she really deserve it for going out just once? What if she promised not to do it again?

But she had made a fool of him! He had believed her story and now he felt like a complete idiot.

As Evergrow sat against the wall, lost in his thoughts, he slowly became aware of a sound. He listened. The Bass Bell was ringing. It was the deepest, most solemn bell in the House, and it sent out a low, chilling, doom-laden note. Evergrow had heard it only half a dozen times in his entire life, if that. The last time was on the day Everwise's body had been discovered at the foot of the stairs to the Hall of Puppets.

Evergrow looked up. He didn't know how long he had been sitting there, or how long the bell had been ringing. It must have been a few minutes, at least. No one in the square was standing and talking now. Everyone was moving. They were all heading towards a corner of the square where a covered walkway led to the Silent Cloister. The expressions on their faces were fearful, their voices, as they questioned each other anxiously, full of concern.

Evergrow got up and followed them. The covered walkway was full of Halibuts hurrying to the Silent Cloister. The Cloister itself, when he reached it, was packed, and the noise of frightened Halibuts was deafening. Evergrow caught sight of a striped shirt and found Eversmart under the roof on one side of the Cloister.

'What's going on?' he said.

Eversmart shrugged.

The tolling of the Bell stopped. The silence left a greater sense of doom than the sound of the Bell itself. The Halibuts glanced at each other, wondering what was to come next.

Suddenly the window in the Great Tower above the roof of the Cloister was thrown open. In it stood the Butler's son, the Younger Digby. He was a small man, like his father, but not yet bent and rheumy with age. He was flanked by Tobias Hildegrew and the three UnderButlers.

A hush descended over the Cloister.

'Halibuts,' said the Younger Digby nervously. 'I have the grave duty to tell you . . .'

A panicky voice rang out from the Cloister. *'He's wearing the Green Coat!'*

'The Green Coat!' cried another voice, and in an instant, the Halibuts were in uproar. There were cries, there were groans. The younger Digby struggled to be heard. Behind him, the UnderButlers exchanged glances. In the Cloister, consternation was turning to panic. People were starting to shake. There was going to be a stampede.

Suddenly a voice rang out above the din. 'Halibuts! Be calm! Be calm!'

Tobias Hildegrew had stepped forward. He held up his arms. The noise died down. The crowd gazed at the window fearfully. The silence was fragile. The slightest fright would set them off again.

'Ladies and gentlemen,' said Hildegrew. 'All will be well. Be calm. All is well.' He paused. 'As you have noticed, yes, Mr Digby is wearing the Green Coat. A sad event has taken place. A terrible accident. He is no longer the *Younger* Mr Digby.'

There were gasps in the Cloister, but Tobias Hildegrew continued to stand in the window with a reassuring, calming air.

'The late Butler, Mr Digby, was found dead this morning.

148

Sad news for us all, for I think there was no one among us who did not love and respect him. But Halibuts, the House is safe. There is no danger. There is no cause for concern. The traditions of the House tell us what will happen. All will continue as before. The House has its Butler. A new Butler, yes, but one who has learned to buttle from his father, who learned from his father before him. All is well. I repeat, we have a Butler. I present him to you. Now he will speak to us. Let us listen.'

He turned to the Younger Digby, who glanced at him questioningly. Tobias Hildegrew reassured him with a nod. The Younger Digby stepped forward again.

'An accident has taken place,' he began. 'A freakish accident. My father . . .' He paused, and almost broke down. Tobias put his hand on the shoulder for a moment and Digby nodded to himself, and clenched his jaw and continued.

But most of the crowd wasn't listening. The Halibuts were all much calmer. In their minds, the old Butler had been replaced by the new Butler and that was enough. As Halibuts, they assumed the new Digby would simply get on and do his job so they could continue living their lives as before. Just as they had almost worked each other into a mindless panic two minutes earlier, now that order had been restored, their thoughts immediately returned to their own concerns.

'Another funeral!' grumbled someone in front of Evergrow. It was Eversniff T Halibut, a man with hair like steel wool who was a notorious grump. 'We'll all be expected to go. Honestly, haven't we got better things to do?'

'Exactly,' said Farinia Halibut, a very pale-skinned lady who was obsessed with cupcakes and everything to do with them. She had five cupcake ovens in her private kitchen and held a cupcake party just about every afternoon. 'I was planning a cupcake party.'

'I've got nothing against a Butler dying after his Captain,' muttered Eversniff irritably. 'Perfectly respectable thing to do. But he could have had the decency to do it at the feast after reading the will! That's when it's supposed to happen. Not a week later.'

'At least there'll be another feast,' said Everfull Halibut, who excelled on such occasions.

'I won't cancel my party,' said Farinia. 'I simply will not.'

'Butler's funerals are at night,' growled Eversniff.

'I might be giving my party at night,' retorted Farinia, who had never given a night-time cupcake party in her life. 'Why not? I very well might be. You'd come, wouldn't you, Kyrelia?' she said to a lady who happened to be standing next to her.

The lady whispered something.

'What was that?'

The lady whispered again, but still no one could hear her. Kyrelia Halibut hardly ever said anything in a voice louder than a whisper, and always dressed in a plain, dark dress, with her hair gathered in a plain, dark bun, as if all she wanted was to avoid being noticed.

'We'll come,' said Everfull.

'When is it?' asked his wife, Insatia.

'Well, it was meant to be on the night of the Butler's funeral, wasn't it?' replied Farinia bitterly. 'But now he's gone and ruined it by dying!'

All around the Cloister, similar conversations were taking place. The Younger Digby tried to speak over the noise of the Halibuts' chatter. 'As for the funeral,' he was saying . . .

Evergrow felt a hand on his shoulder. He looked around. Cornelius Slinker!

The messenger pulled Evergrow back under the roof of the Cloister and pressed him against the wall. He looked quickly from side to side, then bent down, his face close to Evergrow's, his deep-set eyes probing him fiercely.

'Where's Omnia?' he demanded in a harsh whisper.

Evergrow stared. His mouth was dry.

Slinker squeezed his shoulder. 'Where? Do you know?'

Evergrow shook his head. The messenger's face came even closer. His nose was almost touching Evergrow's now. He squeezed his shoulder hard. Evergrow winced.

'You know. Of course you know, you're always together. Where is she? Omnia. Your cousin. You're going to tell me where she is!'

15

The Butler's Funeral

The candles flickered, a ring of twenty yellow lights in the darkness, with one solitary candle in the middle.

The funeral of a Hereditary Butler was unlike that of a Captain of the House, just as the funeral of a servant, in general, was unlike that of a Halibut. It took place at night, in the Meadow of Rest, with candles lighting the coffin. There was no Mourner's Throne and the funeral speech wasn't made in rhyme. And the funeral feast took place in the Captain's Keep, a high, square building not far from the Silent Cloister, and the food consisted not of roasts, but of cakes, muffins and pies, none of which provided any bones for a memorial mound. But one thing was the same. The children, as usual, sat in the trees.

This time Omnia wasn't with them, but she had crept out of Evergrow's room at the time the funeral was scheduled to begin. It would be safe to come out, she thought, because everyone else would have gone to the event. The Hereditary Butler was the only servant whose funeral both servants and Halibuts were expected to attend. From Evergrow's room, Omnia went quickly along the deserted corridor and up the stairs to the roof of the Middle Range. From here, at a corner above the ivy-clad wall, she could see the Meadow of Rest.

The Meadow was dark, like an inky lake. The ring of candles was towards the other side.

Omnia was saddened by the death of the Butler, more saddened than she had been at the death of Everwise. Everyone had always talked respectfully of the Older Digby, which was more than could be said of the Captain. The Butler had also given a picnic each year for the Halibut children on the roof of the Captain's Keep, and had apparently given a separate one each year in the Warren for the children of the servants. As far as Omnia was aware, Everwise had never done anything for anyone. He had even stopped giving his puppet shows in the Hall of Leaning, as if to spite the Halibut children at the cost of his own enjoyment.

Omnia could see the shadows of people standing inside the ring of lights, and she could just make out the dark outline of a coffin. A mass of other shadows stood around the ring, merging with the darkness beyond the reach of the candlelight, and this was all she could see of the throng of servants and Halibuts who had come to see the Butler buried.

But Omnia could see other things from her perch on the roof of the Middle Range. A light moved from window to window in a far-off building, as if someone was walking through a series of rooms, then disappeared. Yet everyone was supposed to be at the funeral. If she herself had been at the funeral – as she certainly would have been had so many extraordinary events not been occurring – she wouldn't have seen the light, and would have thought everyone else was there, just as they were supposed to be. Obviously someone wasn't.

Omnia was reminded of something Basilica had said – *there were things in Neversuch House that no one spoke of.* A funeral like this would be the perfect time if you wanted to do such things.

Another light moved somewhere else in the House, and was gone.

Below, in the Meadow of Rest, the funeral continued. Omnia couldn't make out the details of the ceremony, but the scene was exactly as it had been for the funeral of the previous Butler, and the Butler before him, and every Butler back to the original Digby who had served the First Captain and had died at his feast.

Within the ring of candles stood a dark coffin, and beside it was the new Hereditary Butler, dressed in his father's green velvet coat, holding a candle and reading a speech commemorating his father's Butlership. Two days ago he had been the Younger Digby and could wear whatever he liked, and suddenly he found himself the Older Digby in the long coat of the Hereditary Butler, with all the obligations and responsibilities of the position.

The twenty candles around him were solemnly held by the twenty senior servants of the House, the High Chef, the Chief Mason, the Major Pruner, the First Carpenter, the Prime Plumber, the Grand Glazier and others, all wearing the ceremonial clothes of their profession. Alongside the new Butler inside the ring of candles sat his mother on a Mourner's Throne, and on the other side of the grave stood his closest assistants, in this case, the three UnderButlers and Tobias Hildegrew.

The fact that Tobias, who as yet held no official position, was within the ring made the UnderButlers extremely nervous. There was no required number of UnderButlers that a Butler must have, and in the past some Butlers had had as many as six. Some had one. For years, Trimbleby, Withers and Dish had feared that Tobias Hildegrew, who was nothing more in their eyes than an upstart messenger, would be favoured when the Younger Digby came to power and would become a kind of OverUnderButler, more powerful than any of them. Almost since the moment the old Butler's death had been discovered on the previous day, they had guarded the Butler's office, ensuring the new Butler didn't enter with Hildegrew and look through the old Butler's papers without one of them being present. And since none of them trusted each other any more than they trusted Hildegrew, that meant they had all been guarding his office together, and had even eaten and slept there the previous night.

Now they were continuously glancing at one another and at Hildegrew as the new Butler read his speech and the candles flickered in the hands of the senior servants, while the shadowy crowds of Halibuts and servants look on.

But on the roof of the Middle Range, Omnia knew nothing of this. She was unable to distinguish Digby from the UnderButlers or the UnderButlers from Tobias Hildegrew, much less see the suspicious glances they were giving. Yet still she watched, gazing at the flickering circle of lights and seeing a shadow moving here or there, unable to hear anything that was being said, but knowing that the last words were being spoken over the old Butler's coffin and soon he would be lowered into the ground.

It was good to be outside, at least. Omnia had spent that day, like the day before, hiding in Evergrow's room. Evergrow had come back the previous day to tell her about the Older Digby's death and how it had happened, which he had heard from various people after the crowd in the Silent Cloister dispersed. He also told her about the way Cornelius Slinker had cornered him. Evergrow said he hadn't revealed anything to Cornelius – but he had a few questions of his own!

Was the rumour true? *Had* she been outside the wall? *Did* she go out through the gap in the wall? Evergrow demanded to know the truth. Omnia denied the rumour but she saw the uncertainty in Evergrow's eyes. She couldn't blame him for doubting her. The idea that she had been outside the wall, incredible as it was, must have seemed a lot more believable than her own story about being thrown off the Slate Tower and being caught in a net. If someone had told her that one, she probably would have laughed. In fact, when she thought about it, Evergrow's willingness to believe her did make her wonder whether something had happened to his brain. Yet she had no other way to account for herself that day until the moment she appeared at his window, which would obviously have been more than enough time for her to go beyond the wall and to make her way back.

How could she prove that she was telling the truth? Omnia had shown Evergrow the room she had found beyond his wardrobe, as if to demonstrate that there were things in Neversuch House he didn't know about, sometimes only as far away as a thin wall of plaster. But that still didn't prove she hadn't been outside the wall. And it certainly didn't prove she had been saved from death by being netted in mid-air.

Omnia believed her cousin when he said he hadn't told Slinker where she was. And Evergrow was still letting her hide in his wardrobe. But it was possible Evergrow would tell someone, Omnia knew, if she couldn't find a way of convincing him that she was telling the truth. He might feel he had an obligation to tell someone. If she had been in his shoes, she might well have felt the same.

As for the rumour itself, Omnia knew exactly what to make of it. It was just as Basilica had predicted – if her attacker couldn't find her, he would do something else. This was it. Omnia felt as if she was in a game of chess and her opponent had just made a move. And not just any move. It was smart, she had seen that at once, threatening to bring the game to its end. Instead of merely a few people wondering where she had got to – her parents, for instance, and possibly not even them – now everyone in the House would be on the lookout for her. If she was sighted, word would spread through the House like wildfire and everyone would hear of it, including Cornelius Slinker. And if anything unusual happened in the House, suspicion would fall on her because apparently she had been outside the wall where she had no business to be.

And in the mean time, Slinker was busily trying to find her in case she didn't appear of her own accord.

But what about the death of Digby? Was the Butler's death another part of this whole thing or coincidence? Cornelius Slinker, if that was who her adversary was, had been prepared to kill her, so murder wasn't beyond him. Yet it was one thing to murder an unimportant child, even if she was a Halibut, and another thing entirely to murder the Hereditary Butler of the House.

According to the story Evergrow had heard, the Butler had died in an extraordinary accident, even a freakish one. He fell off his horse and hit his head on a rock, and as he lost consciousness, he rolled face down into a puddle. Not just any puddle, but one that filled a deep rut that should have been fixed months ago. If the knock on the head hadn't killed him instantly, lying face down in a puddle while unconscious would have finished the job. In a word, the Butler drowned.

But that could happen, thought Omnia. Why not? Everyone else apparently thought so. There was no more reason to connect the death of Digby with what was happening to her than there would have been to connect the death of old Everwise, which everyone agreed had been an accident as well. Everyone except Basilica, perhaps.

Besides, why would anyone kill the Butler? What was the motive? She couldn't see how anyone would benefit from the death of the Older Digby, apart from the Younger Digby, who was going to get the Butlership anyway at some point, and had never shown any impatience to get started. Quite the opposite. Who else could have a reason to kill him? Whereas on the other hand, accidents do happen – even freakish ones.

The rumour about her going outside the wall though, that was definitely the work of her attacker. It had to be. And it had trapped her. Anything she said now would be doubted because of what she was believed to have done. Even more than before, she needed proof of what Cornelius Slinker was doing. And proof was the one thing she still lacked.

Far off, in one of the darkened buildings of the House, a light moved. It went past one window, and another, and another, and then disappeared. Someone was out there, someone who should have been at the funeral. Again, Omnia thought of Basilica. There was so much Basilica seemed to know, and so little that she had said.

In the Meadow of Rest, a number of figures were

159

stepping forward into the ring of candles. Omnia could see the figures raise the coffin and then slowly lower it into the grave. Then they stepped back.

'Goodbye, Digby,' murmured Omnia. 'Thanks for the picnics.'

Was his death an accident? People had said that her own near-death under the tile that fell in the Hall of Leaning was an accident, a freakish one, and she knew that wasn't true. And what would they have said if she had been found dead at the bottom of the Slate Tower? What explanation would they have made up? That she had gone to the top of the Tower at six in the morning to explore, perhaps. That she had foolishly stood on top of the waist-high wall to get a better view of something. And that just as she did, a gust of wind had come along and blown her off the Tower.

And people might have believed it, just as they believed the extraordinary story that Evergrow had told her about the way the Butler had died. An accident, they might have said about her death. Not even a freakish one, merely unfortunate.

The lights in the Meadow of Rest bobbed and then the ring of candles dissolved itself into a line, and the line of lights began to move across the inky blackness of the Meadow, as if floating, accompanied by a throng of shadows to left and right, headed in the direction of the Captain's Keep, where the funeral feast of muffins and cakes was waiting.

Omnia watched them go. Soon the candles disappeared and the Meadow of Rest was utterly dark. Somewhere down there, she thought, the Older Digby lay in his coffin at the bottom of his grave, victim of an accident or perhaps something worse.

There were things that happened in Neversuch House that no one talked about, Basilica had said.

Omnia needed to know more. And despite her doubts, Basilica was the only person in all of Neversuch House she could think of to help her.

16

Into Thin Air

Omnia crept out of the wardrobe. Only the faintest hint of light, the first tinge of dawn, filtered around the edges of the curtain. She slipped noiselessly across the room.

'*Where are you going?*'

Omnia froze, hand on the door knob.

Evergrow sat up in bed. 'Omnia, where are you going?'

'Don't worry,' she whispered. 'Go back to sleep.'

Evergrow turned on the light. His hair stood up in tufts on his head and he was wearing blue flannel pyjamas buttoned to the neck. But there was nothing comical in his expression. 'Are you going outside the wall again?'

'I told you,' said Omnia, 'I didn't go outside the wall.'

'Then where are you going?'

'It doesn't matter.'

'Yes it does!' Evergrow stopped, knowing that he might wake his mother and brothers if he spoke too loudly. He whispered. 'How do I know you didn't go outside the wall? How do I know that's not where you're going now?'

'Because I'm not.'

'It's that hole in the wall. That's how you got out, isn't it?'

'*I didn't . . . go . . . out!*' whispered Omnia, fiercely stressing each word. She came closer to Evergrow's bed. Evergrow watched her, eyes narrowed. 'Did you tell anyone I was here?'

Evergrow shook his head. 'I told you I didn't.'

'*Did* you?'

'No! But I could. Maybe I will.'

Omnia gazed at him, trying to decide whether he was telling the truth. 'I thought I could trust you,' she whispered eventually.

'I thought I could trust *you*.'

'I told you what happened. I told you where I was that day.'

'Do you expect me to believe that story?'

'It's true.'

'It's unbelievable.'

'It happened!' Omnia's gaze was fierce. She struggled to keep her voice down. 'Evergrow, do you think I'd make something like that up? Who'd believe it?'

'No one.'

'Exactly! Think about it. If I was making something up, the last thing I'd invent would be something so unbelievable.'

Evergrow watched her doubtfully.

Omnia wondered about him. They had grown up together, they were more like sister and brother than cousins. She had thought she could trust him with anything. But maybe there was a limit to trust, even with Evergrow. Maybe these events had taken her past it. And who could blame him? If she had been in Evergrow's place, the limit probably would have been passed long before.

She sat down on the bed beside him. 'Evergrow, if I can't trust you to believe me, there's no one I can trust. So tell me now. Tell me if I can trust you. If I can't, I'll walk out that door and find somewhere to hide by myself.'

Evergrow's eyes narrowed.

'Evergrow?'

He hesitated for a moment. 'Take me with you.'

Omnia shook her head.

'Then you *are* going outside the wall.'

'I'm not.'

'Then prove it. Take me with you.' Evergrow got up. He went to the wardrobe and opened the door. 'I'm going to get changed. If you're not here when I come out, I'll know what to do.'

He closed the door behind him. Omnia stared at the closed door, then shook her head in frustration. She had no choice. She folded her arms and waited.

Five minutes later, she and Evergrow poked their heads out of the east door of the Middle Range. Omnia had brought a blanket with her and she hooded herself with it, as if protecting herself from the dawn cold. They looked around for a moment, came out and hurried away.

But they didn't look carefully enough. As soon as they had moved off, a tall, dark figure unfolded himself from deep within the shadows of a doorway where he had been sitting, curled up, watching. The person stretched, pulled the black hood of his cloak over his head and set off after them at an almost noiseless trot.

The cool air in the Great Kitchen Court was scented with the smell of fresh-baked bread. A kitchen boy came out of a doorway carrying a bucket of pig's trotters in each hand. Another kitchen boy emerged from a different doorway with a sheep's carcase slung over his shoulder. Omnia went quickly past them, head hooded by her blanket, face averted. She led Evergrow up the stairs to the Pale Octangle, then round a corner and down a set of stairs that brought them close to the Bright Tower and led to the clustered buildings beyond.

In the Echo Walk, the sounds of their footsteps rose to a crescendo and thundered around their ears. Then they came out and the noise was gone. Or was it? Omnia stopped. 'Wait here a second,' she whispered.

She took a step back into the Echo Walk. Sounds came from the other end. They grew. Footsteps.

Omnia came out quickly. 'Let's go!' she whispered, and set off at a run.

Evergrow ran after her. They took a set of stairs, crossed

the terrace at the top, then ran to the two reapers and climbed the stairs above them. Omnia turned left and then stopped for a moment. Now that she knew what she was listening for, she could hear them. Footsteps were coming quickly up the stairs. Omnia and Evergrow ran again. Under an arch, left, left once more, and then they were in the courtyard with the four coloured houses around them. They ran into the Blue House. Evergrow stopped in the entrance hall, gazing at the coloured tiles and bricks and carpets and marble all around him. Omnia pulled his arm. 'Come on!' she cried, and leaped up the stairs.

She stopped at the top, breathing heavily, waiting for Evergrow, who arrived a few seconds later.

From the top landing, Omnia looked down over the railing at the empty entrance hall below. 'Go,' she whispered to Evergrow, pointing to the yellow door that led to the walkway to the Slate Tower. 'Wait out there.'

Evergrow went out the door. Omnia stayed on the landing, standing back from the railing, listening.

At first there was silence. Then she heard footsteps on the marble of the entrance hall. Cautiously, Omnia peered over the railing. A black, hooded figure stood below her, in the middle of the hall, looking around. Then slowly, he put his head back and gazed upward.

The hood fell back.

Cornelius Slinker.

Omnia felt a flood of ice in her veins, all the way to her fingertips. Her skin prickled, as if the two hands that had clutched her at the top of the Slate Tower were clutching her again.

He saw her.

'Omnia Halibut!' called Slinker.

She ran. Through the yellow door and out on the walkway where she almost collided with Evergrow. 'Come on!' she cried. She raced to the door of the Slate Tower. Evergrow ran after her. She climbed the spiral stairs. Up she went, upwards and upwards, the stairs always curving away into more stairs. Her legs were aching. Still she climbed. Finally she came out on to the turret. Evergrow came out as well.

He leaned against the wall of the turret, gasping for air.

Omnia went back inside the door and listened. She heard footsteps. Slinker was coming after her. He was on the staircase.

Omnia came out and climbed on the parapet.

Evergrow stared at her in disbelief.

'I'll go first,' she said. 'Wait a minute and come after me.'

Evergrow glanced down at the sheer drop in terror.

'Basilica!' she yelled. 'It's Omnia. Here I come!'

'Omnia!' cried Evergrow. 'You don't really believe she'll catch you again!'

For a final second, Omnia hesitated, wondering just that. Then she hugged her arms around her chest, closed her eyes and stepped off the parapet into thin air.

17

Breakfast with Basilica

Omnia bounced, jiggled, and then she was over the sill and inside, sprawling on the floor.

'Quick!' she said. 'There's someone else coming.'

'I don't need anyone else,' replied Basilica. 'I've caught quite enough today. Any more would be greedy'

'But he's *coming*!' cried Omnia. *'Now! Please, Basilica!'*

'Oh, all right.' Basilica put her net out the window and an instant later something plummeted out of the sky. She hauled Evergrow in and tipped him out on the rug.

'Anyone else?' inquired Basilica impatiently.

Omnia shook her head.

'I thought you weren't going to tell anyone else about me.'

'I'm sorry, it's just . . . he's my cousin.'

Basilica shook her head, giving Omnia a look of dissatisfaction, and then turned to Evergrow.

He was sitting on the floor, watching them in disbelief.

'See?' Omnia said to him. 'Do you believe me now?'

'Did he not?' demanded Basilica. 'If I'd known that before I'd caught you,' she said to Evergrow, 'I wouldn't have bothered.'

'I don't think we should blame him,' said Omnia. 'I'm not sure if I would have believed it either.'

Basilica shrugged. 'I should warn you, young man, that if you mention me to anyone else, you'll be sorry.' She glanced at Omnia. 'Did you tell anybody else?'

Omnia shook her head.

'Promise?'

'Yes.'

'All right. It's for your own good. You too,' said Basilica, turning back to Evergrow. 'And in case you're wondering, I don't normally catch just anything that happens to be falling outside my window. I would probably have left you alone if Omnia hadn't asked me to.'

'Thank you,' murmured Evergrow. He was still almost dumb with fear and amazement.

'I wouldn't advise you to try your luck like that again.'

Evergrow shook his head.

'Good. Have you got a name?'

'Evergrow D Halibut.'

'He's Ribelia's son,' said Omnia, knowing what question was bound to come next.

'Is he just? I was never really very friendly with Ribelia.'

Basilica glanced at Omnia. 'I don't know why. We just didn't get on.'

'I suppose that happens,' said Omnia, settling into an armchair.

'Yes, it does. She used to knit. Does she still knit?'

Evergrow nodded.

Omnia grinned. 'He's got a whole wardrobe full of stuff.

'It's not that bad,' said Evergrow.

Omnia laughed. 'You never wear any of it!'

'What about other things?' said Basilica. 'She used to knit enormous, complicated things. Kettles and saucepans, I seem to remember. Couldn't use them of course. I never saw the point.'

'She's never tried to knit a kettle!' said Evergrow.

'Hasn't she just? When she was younger, your mother did all kinds of things. You should ask her one day.' Basilica looked at him knowingly. 'Peculiar thing, knitting.'

'Not as peculiar as someone fishing for birds,' muttered Evergrow.

'Well, you should be happy I do! Or else right now you'd be a small flat splat at the bottom of the Tower and Omnia here would have to go down and scrape you up. Ever seen someone after they've splattered from a fall like that?' Basilica peered at him expectantly. 'No, and you wouldn't want to, either.' She paused. 'Well, get up! You're here now. You don't need to stay on the floor. Find yourself a chair.'

Evergrow looked around at all the chairs in the room,

170

then glanced at Omnia, who shrugged. He sat down beside her.

There was silence. Basilica glanced at Omnia, and at Evergrow, and back at Omnia.

'I need to ask you a question,' said Omnia.

Basilica waited.

'Someone started a rumour about me. People are saying I was seen outside the wall.'

'That's not a question,' said Basilica. 'Is it true, by the way?'

Omnia shook her head.

'Well, it's obvious who started it, isn't it?'

Omnia nodded.

Basilica smiled thoughtfully. 'A rumour that you've been outside the wall. Clever. I hadn't thought of that. That's very clever.'

'Something else has happened,' said Omnia. 'The Butler's dead.'

'The Butler? How?'

'Haven't you heard?' asked Evergrow.

'If I'd heard, I wouldn't ask, would I? Do you know how he died?'

'It was a freakish accident,' said Evergrow, and he told her the main facts of the case as he had heard them.

'Astonishing,' said Basilica. 'Fell off the horse, knocked his head, rolled into a puddle, lost consciousness and drowned. Truly astonishing. But do you know what an even more astonishing thing is?'

Neither of the two children answered.

'That the person who saw all this apparently didn't bother to help. Personally, if I saw that happen, I'd have done something. I don't think I would have let him drown.'

'No one actually saw it,' said Evergrow.

'Ah.' Basilica nodded knowingly. 'No one saw it.'

'But everyone agrees that's how it must have happened from how he was found.'

'Then perhaps we should think about how he was found. Let's look at the facts, Evergrow, before we turn to the interpretation. Tell me *everything* you've heard.'

Evergrow told her. The first sign that something was wrong was when the Butler's horse, on which he customarily rode around the estate surrounding the buildings of the House, had been found running free, still saddled, in the Great Kitchen Court. One of the stable hands reported helping the Butler get on, which was the last time anyone saw him alive. Shortly afterwards, the Butler had been discovered near the entrance of the alley that ran along the side of the West Stable, lying face down in the rut that was full of water. He had a huge wound at the back of his head, and the corner of the gutter beside the puddle was covered in blood. The Butler had been far too old and arthritic to go riding around the estate by himself, and had been told so many times by Eldred Sturgeon, yet he persisted in doing it. This wasn't the first fall that he had had.

'That's very sad,' said Basilica quietly, when Evergrow

had finished. 'I didn't dislike Digby, although heaven knows I had a right to. After a while, you can forgive even if you can't forget. He wasn't the worst of them, that's for sure. Everything he did, he did because he thought it was best for the House, at least by his own understanding. That's something one can respect.' Basilica paused, frowning, perhaps at some memory that was going through her mind. She shook her head. 'Sad he should end up being murdered.'

Evergrow stared at her in astonishment.

'What?' said Basilica. 'You don't believe that ridiculous story about him falling off his horse and rolling into a puddle, do you? You look like such intelligent children. What about you, Omnia?'

'Apparently everyone else believes it.'

'All the more reason not to.'

'But it could be true,' said Evergrow.

'It could, I agree. But the probability is low. No, I fear the story of how Digby died is somewhat different. Far less extraordinary and far more brutal. He got off his horse. Someone then knocked him down and smashed his head against the gutter, knocking him out. Then they turned him face down in the puddle and held him down until they were sure he was dead.'

'But how could anyone have got him off his horse?' demanded Evergrow. 'Why would he have got off? They'd have to have chased him, they'd have to have pulled him down. Why didn't he shout? Why didn't he scream?'

'Very dramatic,' remarked Basilica drily. 'I'm sure he

would have screamed if any of that had happened. And yet it didn't.'

'Because?'

'Because he trusted his murderer,' said Omnia. 'That's what you mean, isn't it?'

Basilica nodded. 'If you know your murderer, if you trust him, you don't scream, do you? You don't realise until it's too late.'

Evergrow glanced at Omnia and grimaced.

'Why?' said Omnia.

'Why would anyone kill him?' said Basilica. 'Is that the question you came here to ask me?'

Omnia nodded.

'Maybe they didn't like him.'

Omnia shook her head. She wasn't persuaded. 'Why now?'

'What do you mean now?'

'After the Captain dies. If someone didn't like him they could have killed him any time. It's too much of a coincidence.'

Basilica smiled. 'I agree.'

'But you just said—' Evergrow stopped. Basilica was looking at him with one eyebrow raised. 'Oh, I see,' said Evergrow. 'You were just testing us, weren't you?'

'Have you ever noticed how often in our history the Butler has died just after the Captain?' said Basilica. 'Five times. Three at the funeral feast, on two other occasions within a week. This makes a sixth. Six times out of ten.'

'But that's coincidence, right?' said Evergrow. He looked at Omnia. 'That's what she means, isn't it?'

'Omnia, the Hereditary Butler wears a key around his neck. Did you know that? Every minute of every day.'

'A key?' said Omnia. 'You're saying someone murdered him so they could take a key? But if he was murdered, and the key was taken, surely that would be the first thing to be noticed.'

'It wouldn't need to be taken,' said Basilica. 'Let's return to the scene of the crime. Digby lies face down in the puddle, dead from the blow on the head or from drowning – who can say? The assassin rolls him over, opens his shirt, takes hold of the key and makes an impression of it – in wax, or a soft piece of clay, or some other substance. This takes all of . . . ten seconds. The impression made, he closes Digby's shirt, rolls him over again and leaves. When the body is found, the key is still there. But now the assassin can forge a copy, here, in the House, or in the Warren, in some remote room with a secret forge that he's constructed, or in the city, if he chooses to leave.'

'If he can go and come back without suspicion,' said Omnia.

'Exactly. Now let me tell you something else. There's a second key. Can you guess around whose neck it hangs?'

The hairs on Omnia's neck prickled. 'The Captain's?'

Basilica nodded. 'One key hangs around the neck of the Hereditary Butler, the other around the neck of the Captain of the House. By itself, each one is useless. Together, they open the door to the Halibut treasure.'

The two children stared at Basilica, eyes wide with awe.

'In the Great Tower?' asked Omnia softly.

'So they say. Don't you understand yet, Omnia? You should never believe anything that's said about Neversuch House.'

There was silence. Omnia stared at the rug on the floor, thinking. She looked up at Basilica. 'Do you think the same thing happened to Everwise? You think someone killed him, don't you?'

Basilica shrugged. 'Accidents happen. One, possibly. But two? So quickly? And we know for certain that someone is trying to kill you as well. That would have looked like an accident as well, wouldn't it? A third one.' Basilica shook her head. 'Accidents . . . If you knew the history of the House, the real history, you'd find a lot more accidents than you'd expect.'

'If someone was able to take a copy of the key that Everwise wore, he'll have them both.'

'Well, if he's got them,' said Evergrow, 'at least you're safe, Omnia. He doesn't need to get rid of you any more.'

'On the contrary,' replied Basilica. 'Omnia's less safe than ever. He's started the rumour to discredit Omnia in case she comes forward. That will buy him time, he hopes, to get what he needs. He kills the Butler and copies the key. But now he must wait. The UnderButlers will be suspicious. Two deaths like this? In public, they might tell everyone they were accidents, but the UnderButlers aren't stupid. In private, they'll have their doubts. They'll be taking precautions to keep the treasure safe, not to mention the Captain and the new Butler. If the killer has the keys, it will be too dangerous for him to use them now. They'll be ready for him. Traps will have been set in case he tries to use them. So he must bide his time until things settle down, everything goes back to normal, no one's suspicious, then use the keys when it's safer. Perhaps in a month, perhaps in a year. But in the mean time, he fears that Omnia will identify him. She's the last obstacle in his way. Every moment that she lives she poses a threat. So he must get her, Evergrow. Don't you see? This changes nothing. He won't stop until he has.'

Omnia gazed at the rug again. She could see Cornelius Slinker's face, gazing up at her from the bottom of the stairs, revealed by the hood that had fallen from his head. But no one else had seen him, only her. Evergrow had already been outside on the walkway to the tower.

'Now,' said Basilica cheerfully, getting up and opening a small door in the wood panelling that covered the walls. 'Would anyone like breakfast?'

The table was laden with food. There were pies and sausages and cakes and tarts, savoury and sweet. And a formally dressed man with thick grey hair, waxy skin, and black, owl-like eyebrows. One of which he raised as Omnia and Evergrow came through.

'Don't mind Winnicott,' remarked Basilica. 'He's perfectly trustworthy.'

The man nodded gravely.

Omnia stared at the food. It was an odd collection of food for breakfast. And so much of it!

'I had a feeling you might be dropping in again,' said Basilica 'Always best to be prepared.'

Prepared for about forty people from the look of it, thought Omnia.

'The fishing has been excellent recently,' Basilica added.

Evergrow reached to take a piece of pie.

Winnicott coughed loudly.

'Winnicott will serve,' said Basilica. 'It's his job.'

Winnicott nodded. He stepped forward and pulled out a chair for Omnia and one for Evergrow. Then he placed the piece of pie Evergrow had been taking on a plate and put it in front of him. Without hesitation, Evergrow dug in.

'For the young lady?' inquired Winnicott.

Omnia looked at the food suspiciously.

Basilica sat down opposite her. 'Just a slice of the pigeon for me, Winnicott.'

Winnicott cut a slice of pigeon pie and put it on a plate for Basilica. Then he turned to Omnia again.

'What's that?' asked Omnia, pointing at a pie from which one piece was missing.

'Bat,' replied Winnicott. 'Very good, if I may say so.' He brushed a crumb away from the corner of his mouth.

'What about that one?'

178

'Green parrot.'

'And that?'

'Red. Highly recommended.' Winnicott cut a slice and held it out on the knife over Omnia's plate, a questioning look in his eye.

'All right,' said Omnia.

Winnicott nodded and put the slice on her plate. 'Chutney?'

'I suppose so.' Omnia watched as Winnicott set a spoonful of green chutney on the plate beside the pie. Then she looked at Basilica, who took a forkful of the pie on her plate. Omnia did likewise.

It wasn't bad. Not bad at all. With each mouthful it tasted better. A slightly smoky taste with a hint of spice. Omnia had never imagined that parrot would be so delicious.

Evergrow had just about finished his first piece of pie and was already eyeing the table for a second.

Suddenly Omnia felt ravenous. For two days, in Evergrow's room, she had eaten only the jam rolls and muffins that he had brought her. She followed the red parrot pie with a pair of duck sausages, a sparrow pasty, a piece of the pigeon pie that Basilica had eaten, followed by goose liver on toast and a red robin tart. Everything was excellent. Evergrow did just as much damage, and yet the table was still laden with provisions, and they could have eaten four times as much again and still hardly have made a dent in the food.

Basilica, who took only the one piece of pie, waited until they were finished.

'I want to show you something,' she said.

She took them to a window.

'Look down there. What do you see?'

Far below them, entirely enclosed within a wall, was a small, diamond-shaped garden. Hedges ran in intricate patterns, cutting meticulous shapes, and the small areas of lawn between them were facets of perfect green. The garden was like a beautiful green jewel, and the wall that enclosed it was its clasp.

'Have either of you ever seen that garden before?'

Omnia and Evergrow shook their heads.

'Yet there it is. And I promise you, if you tried to find the way in, you never would.'

'Who uses it?' asked Omnia.

'It doesn't matter. Omnia, no one knows everything that's in this House. The gardens, the rooms, the passages, the tunnels. Somewhere, there's a whole forest inside a building, with a roof of glass to let in the sun. Did you know that? And there's an underground river. Entirely underground! Have either of you ever heard of it?'

They shook their heads again.

'No, nor had my father until he discovered it. He used to take me and my brother in a gondola and sing operas for us when I was small. He would paddle us slowly down the river with a lantern on the gondola to light the way, and he would paddle us slowly back, and his voice would echo off the walls. I would lie back and look at the cracks of the rock in the ceiling. They were just like pictures.' Basilica was silent for

180

a moment, remembering. 'My father had a wonderful voice. He often gave recitals in the Purple Nave for anyone who wanted to come, but the trips on the underground river were just for us. I don't think I could even remember how to get there, I was so little at the time, and I don't know if anyone knows today. I don't know how my father discovered it. Yet the river's there, and if it's been forgotten, one day someone will discover it again. Who knows? Maybe the gondola's still there, where my father left it. That's what the House is like. No one knows everything that it contains. Sometimes I wonder whether the First Captain himself knew everything that was being built here.'

'How could he not?' asked Evergrow. 'He had the plans.'

'Perhaps he told some of his masons to build things as they wanted and not let him know. To surprise him.'

'You mean like the room at the back of my wardrobe?'

'It was sealed off,' explained Omnia. It wasn't the kind of secret place Basilica meant because it had looked as if it had once been open and someone had used it, and only after that had it been sealed off. 'I found it behind the wall in Evergrow's wardrobe. And I found a picture of you.'

Basilica stared.

'It's you, when you were young. I'm sure it's you.'

'Where is this?' Basilica's voice was barely above a whisper. She turned to Evergrow. 'Where do you live?'

'In the Middle Range.'

'What floor?'

'Third.'

'And is there a chest of drawers in this room? The one you found, Omnia. Is there a big chest, against the wall?'

Omnia nodded.

Basilica was silent. Omnia glanced at Winnicott. The servant was watching her from under his thick, beetling brows.

'There's another picture of you with a man,' she said to Basilica.

'How old is he?'

'Young. You're both smiling.' Omnia had an idea. 'You just mentioned that you have a brother. Is it him?'

Basilica didn't reply. Omnia watched her. The pictures were of Basilica, she was sure. And Basilica knew that room. She knew it contained a chest of drawers. At some point in the past, long ago, she had been there.

'Who's your brother?' asked Omnia. 'What's his name?'

'Doesn't matter,' whispered Basilica. 'You'd never have heard of him.'

'Why not? What happened? Is he dead?'

Basilica was silent. Suddenly she gripped Omnia's wrist. 'Things are happening, Omnia. The death of a Captain is a dangerous time. The House is vulnerable. First the Captain dies, then the Butler. The forces are in motion, Omnia. Don't you see? The forces are in motion again.'

'There's a bird,' said Evergrow. 'A great black condor that's been flying at night since Everwise died.'

'Is there?' said Basilica.

'It flies above the Great Tower. People say it's a sign.'

'What of?'

Evergrow shrugged. 'Do you think it's a sign?'

'I don't know what it is.' Basilica paused. She turned to Omnia again. 'I have a question for you, Omnia. Have you ever heard of the Evergones?'

Omnia shook her head. She noticed Winnicott out of the corner of her eye. A look of concern, almost fear, had come over his face.

'Who are they?' said Omnia.

Winnicott coughed quickly.

Basilica glanced at him. 'I haven't *said* anything, Winny!'

'You're very close,' murmured the servant.

'They can make exceptions.'

'*They* – not you.'

Omnia watched them in confusion. She glanced at Evergrow, who was just as puzzled.

'What are you talking about?' she said.

Basilica and Winnicott seemed to be ignoring her. Winnicott shook his head. Basilica watched him for a moment longer.

Suddenly she grasped Omnia's shoulders and crouched to face her. 'Do you know who it is? Do you know who attacked you? You do, don't you?'

Omnia hesitated. 'I've got no proof. It would just be my word against somebody else's.'

'Is it a servant?'

'I think so.'

'That's no good then. They'd never take your word against his.'

'That doesn't sound right!' said Evergrow. 'We're the—'

'What?' demanded Basilica.

'The Halibuts,' said Evergrow. He frowned uncertainly. '*They're* the servants, aren't they?'

Basilica looked at him for a moment, then turned back to Omnia. 'If you don't have proof, you must get it before he gets you.'

'How?'

'You must catch him in the act.'

'What act? How do I know what he'll do next?'

'There's one act you can be sure he'll try to commit.'

Omnia stared at her.

Basilica let go of her shoulders. She stood, gazing thoughtfully at Omnia. 'Every so often a Halibut comes along who *can* do something. Or tries to, at least. Somehow, despite all the odds, every generation produces one.'

'Who was the one in your generation?' asked Omnia quietly.

'It doesn't matter,' said Basilica. 'Whoever she was, it's obvious she didn't succeed.'

There was silence.

Omnia frowned. 'That act he'll try to commit. You mean me, don't you? You mean my murder.'

Basilica nodded. 'He'll come for you, if you let him.'

18

Under the Roof of the Ribbled Lodge

The chimneys loomed out of the darkness like a forest of broken trees. In the moonlight, the roof of the Ribbled Lodge was covered in them, and every one was different.

Omnia counted four chimneys across from the left front corner, as Basilica had instructed her, then two chimneys in, then four more across. The one she had reached had a wide base and rose stepwise to a narrower top, which was what Basilica had described. Omnia climbed a couple of steps and peered inside. Black. There was no way to know how far it was to the bottom.

'You're sure this is the one she meant?' whispered Evergrow.

Omnia hoped so. If not, there was no knowing how far she was going to fall.

She climbed over the edge and lowered herself down until she was hanging by her hands. Then she let go.

Almost immediately she hit a floor. Crouching, she reached down behind her. She felt the rungs of a ladder, as Basilica had said she would.

She called softly to Evergrow. He dropped a bag down the chimney and Omnia caught it. She went down the ladder. A moment later, Evergrow followed.

There was no light in here. Basilica had given them a lantern. Omnia lit it.

It was a big room, oddly shaped, with a high ceiling and bare wooden floor. In the walls and across the ceiling ran enormous wooden beams, as if here, under its skin, the building's skeleton was exposed. The chimney down which they had come didn't end at a fireplace, but at a ledge in the wall just below the roof, from which the ladder descended. In one corner of the room was a tap and a toilet. Provided you had food, you could live in here for weeks, months. But there was no door in the room nor any way to climb back up the chimney from the hole in the wall. The only exit was through one small window.

Outside the window, Basilica had explained, the pattern of the wall provided a kind of ladder down to the ground, with deep handholds and footholds carved in the stone. The ladder was concealed by the roughness of the Lodge's wall, which had been built to look crazily cracked and ribbled. Outside, no one would suspect that a ladder was embedded in the apparently random criss-crossing patterns of the stones. Omnia herself must have passed the wall hundreds of times and never had an inkling of it, nor suspected that a hidden room lay beneath the forest of chimneys on the roof.

Omnia put the lantern down. Evergrow was watching her.

'You're not really going to do it,' he said.

Omnia knew what Evergrow was talking about. After they had left Basilica, as they had waited in the tunnel opposite the Purple Nave for night to fall, she had devised a plan. She had already told Evergrow what it was.

'You *can't* do it!'

Omnia shrugged. She sat down. Evergrow came and knelt in front of her.

'You can't, Omnia! It's too dangerous.'

'You heard what Basilica said.'

'She's insane! She goes fishing for birds.'

'You heard what she said,' muttered Omnia quietly.

'How did she know all that stuff?' demanded Evergrow. 'She could be wrong. It's just a guess. It might have been an accident, both times, the Captain and the Butler.'

Omnia shook her head. It wasn't just a guess. Basilica, she realised, was speaking from some kind of experience. The forces were in motion, she had said. They were in motion *again*.

Basilica must have seen something very similar before, or had heard of it. Omnia wondered whether it had something to do with the fact that she seemed to be locked in that apartment in the Slate Tower, unable to leave.

'Well, I don't care what she knows or doesn't know,' said

Evergrow. 'She should never have said what she said to you!'

'I would have worked it out for myself. To trap someone, you need bait.'

'And you're it, are you?'

'Can you think of anyone else?'

'She's evil, Omnia! She should never have suggested it to you.'

Omnia sighed. 'She didn't suggest it, Evergrow. She simply pointed out the facts – there's only one thing we can be sure of, and that's that the killer will come after me if I let him. What I do about that is up to me. The plan's mine, Evergrow, not hers. And it's the only thing to do.'

Evergrow didn't know what to say to that. He sat against the wall and shook his head in frustration. He began to pick at a splinter in the huge beam that ran up the wall beside him.

Omnia watched him. Evergrow had really surprised her today. It had taken courage to jump off the Tower – more than just courage, which was hardly the word to describe it – even after seeing her get caught in a net. And yet he had done it. Omnia imagined what that must have looked like to him – her falling, then a net suddenly jutting out, catching her and disappearing inside. Even after seeing that, how could you be sure the net would come out again when you jumped? Omnia wouldn't have thought Evergrow would have that much courage in him. Perhaps he was braver than she thought.

Or perhaps he was just so scared of whoever was coming up the stairs after them that jumping seemed the better option. He didn't know for certain at that point that it was Cornelius Slinker – he hadn't been there to see Slinker's face when the messenger looked up from the entrance of the Blue House and Omnia had only told him later, after they had left Basilica – but he probably guessed. Even if that was the case, it took courage to jump.

And he was only thinking of her safety now. But right now, unless she was in hiding, she wasn't safe, and the only one way to change that was to trap her attacker. And the only way to do that was to put herself in danger.

It scared her. Of course it did. Only a fool wouldn't be scared at what she had to do. It wasn't a joke. This wasn't a game and the plan she had come up with wasn't guaranteed to work. It could all go wrong.

'Evergrow, listen. I've told you what I need you to do. Tomorrow you have to go to Digby and tell him that his father was murdered and I know who did it. Tell him I'll reveal who it is if he meets me at midnight in the Silent Cloister. He should come with the UnderButlers. No one else. Tell him if I see he's with anyone else, I'll run away again and he'll never find out who did it. Make sure he understands.'

Omnia looked at Evergrow seriously. If any of the Halibuts found out about her plan, she knew, when midnight came, the Cloister would be ablaze with light and packed with noisy Halibut spectators who had brought picnic baskets and were taking bets on whether the plan would succeed. The only person who wouldn't be there would be the one person she was trying to attract.

'Tomorrow's the Second Night,' said Evergrow.

Omnia frowned. On the second night after the burial of a Butler, the new Butler and all his clerks were required to ceremoniously clean the Butlery. Traditionally, it took all night. Digby and the UnderButlers wouldn't be able to come. 'Make it the night after next,' she said reluctantly. Every day she had to wait was another day of danger.

Evergrow was almost physically ill at the thought of the risk Omnia was going to run. 'Why don't you just tell him? Let's go to the Bright Tower and tell the Butler now.'

'What?'

'That you know who it is.'

'I don't *know* who it is. I suspect. And I've got no proof.'

'You saw him!'

'*I* saw him, no one else. That's not proof. That's just my word against his.'

'So let him prove his innocence.'

'He won't have to. They won't believe me. You heard what Basilica said.'

'She must be wrong. We're Halibuts!'

Omnia shrugged. She had been surprised when Basilica said that her word wouldn't be taken against that of a servant. But even if Basilica was wrong, or was exaggerating, in her case there was an extra problem. 'Supposedly I went outside the wall, remember? That's the whole point of the rumour, to cast doubt on me. Evergrow, face it, no one's going to believe a word I say. They'll just think I'm trying to move suspicion away from myself. And in the mean time, I'll be out there and he'll find me and I'll just happen to die in some kind of freakish accident.' Omnia shook her head. 'There's only one way to do it, Evergrow, and that's to *show* them. To set the trap and have the killer come after me and for them to see it for themselves.'

'You can't do it alone.'

'And if he sees anyone else, he won't come near me. Please, Evergrow, just do as I say. Tell the Butler and the UnderButlers to hide in the Cloister. They need to make sure they can't be seen.'

'Let me at least—'

'No, you can't come with me. We've been through this. I have to be by myself. He has to come after me in the Cloister. The Butler and the UnderButlers have to see it.'

'He can come after both of us.'

'No.'

'He did this morning.'

'This is different. This time we're telling him where to find me. If he thinks it's a trap, he'll stay away. Admit it, Evergrow. He's less likely to think it's a trap if it's just me.'

Evergrow picked at the splinter in frustration, picked and picked at it until a long, sharp sliver of wood came away.

'How do you even know you're safe here?' he demanded. 'Why do you even trust her? How can you, when she's telling you to risk your life? I didn't hear *her* volunteering to come along.'

'It's not her problem.'

'So she can just sit there in her Tower and tell you to get yourself killed.'

'You forget, she saved my life. And yours.'

'Only because we chose to jump.'

'I didn't choose the first time.'

Evergrow was silent.

'Evergrow, I trust her.'

'You didn't before! You came to me when you needed somewhere to hide, remember?'

'I trust her now. So far, everything she's said has been right.' Omnia paused. 'I still need your help.'

'Then let me come with you! You can't do it alone. You can't—'

'I can!'

'Everlook wouldn't let you go by yourself!'

'Everlook's not here!' Omnia sighed. There was no point talking about what their uncle would do because he wasn't there and he was never going to be again. 'Everlook would realise this is exactly what I have to do.'

'He wouldn't let you do it alone.'

'Well, you're not Everlook, are you?'

Evergrow bit his lip.

'I'm sorry, Evergrow. I didn't mean to say that. Really. If you want to help me, just do as I ask. Please. Go to the Butler tomorrow and give him the message.'

There was silence. Evergrow picked at the wood.

'What do we do to murderers?' he asked eventually.

Omnia didn't know. She had never heard of a murder in Neversuch House.

'Perhaps there's never been one,' said Evergrow.

Or one that was detected, thought Omnia. She had lived in Neversuch House for twelve and a quarter years, and until a week ago, she had thought she knew everything about it. Yet now she was beginning to think she hardly knew the first thing. And it wasn't only a matter of hidden rooms and concealed ladders. Basilica had said that nothing was as it seemed in Neversuch House, and Omnia was beginning to understand that she was talking about much more than the architecture.

'I think the condor's a sign,' said Evergrow.

'Do you?' Omnia looked at him doubtfully. Evermay, who had painted its shadow projecting over the whole House, thought it was a sign too. But Omnia didn't believe in signs like that. The events happening in reality were quite extraordinary enough without having to imagine there were signs in the sky as well.

Omnia rested her head against the wall and closed her eyes. She thought of something Basilica had said, and the look on Winnicott's face when she had said it. *The Evergones.* What, or who, were they? They must be important, and it was clear that she wasn't supposed to know about them. Basilica had refused to explain what they were nor given any indication that she would.

193

Omnia opened her eyes and looked around the room. The lantern sent its flickering light over the timbers. The beams were huge, powerful, fissured with age. Omnia knew they must be the very timbers on which the First Captain's workers had set the roof of the Ribbled Lodge when the House was built. The sight was reassuring. For over two hundred years they had stood here, strong and reliable, bearing the weight of the great roof and its forest of chimneys, and there was no reason they would not stand for two hundred more, thought Omnia, and another two hundred after that.

Suddenly Evergrow frowned. 'Omnia, there's one thing you haven't thought of. If I only tell the Butler and the UnderButlers to come to the Cloister, and if I tell them they can't tell anyone else, how's Cornelius Slinker going to hear about it?'

Omnia turned her head. 'You'll have to find a way to tell him as well.'

19

Inside the Bright Tower

The two men sat at a high desk under a huge brass clock. One of them had a moustache and mutton chop whiskers, and the other didn't, and otherwise, there was very little to tell them apart. They both wore the walnut-coloured coats of Butlery clerks, buttoned at the front, with high collars and orange stitching, and they were both writing busily. First one looked up, and then the other, and then they both looked down again and kept writing.

'Excuse me,' said Evergrow. It was the first time he had ever been inside the Bright Tower, which housed the Butlery. Halibuts, as a rule, avoided it and were encouraged to do so. He had climbed a long, narrow flight of stairs and this is what he had found facing the entrance in the room at the top: a desk, a clock and two clerks who seemed to be ignoring him.

'Excuse me,' he said again. 'I'm here to see the Butler.'

The clerk with the whiskers looked up. 'And you are . . . ?'

'Evergrow D Halibut,' replied Evergrow.

'Indeed?' said the clerk, and he glanced at the other clerk, who had looked up again, and they smirked.

'I'm here to see the Butler,' repeated Evergrow.

'Are you really?' muttered the whiskered clerk, and went back to his writing. The other clerk had already gone back to his.

'It's about Omnia Halibut.'

Both the clerks looked up.

'What about Omnia Halibut?' said the whiskered clerk.

'I have information.'

'What information?'

'It's for the Butler.'

'You can tell us.'

Evergrow shook his head.

The clerk narrowed his eyes. 'You can tell us, I said.'

'No,' replied Evergrow. He crossed his arms. 'I'm only telling the Butler.'

'What makes you think the Butler wants to listen to you?'

'I'm a Halibut.'

The two clerks glanced at one another and then they burst into laughter. They were almost crying with amusement. One of them dabbed at his eyes.

Evergrow watched them in dismay. 'I have information about Omnia Halibut! And I'm only going to tell the Butler! Myself, face to face!'

At that, both clerks fell silent again. The whiskered one stood up. He was a big, broad man and his face went red with irritation. 'Are you *just?*' he demanded.

Involuntarily, Evergrow took a couple of steps back. But he managed to nod and then he put his hands on his hips. 'Yes,' he said.

There was silence for a moment. Then the clerk stabbed his finger in the direction of a chair that stood behind Evergrow next to the entrance. 'Wait there,' he said, and left the room by a door behind the desk.

The clerk who remained at the desk glared at him, then turned back to his writing.

Evergrow sat down. Another clerk, whom Evergrow hadn't noticed when he came in, sat on a chair on the other side of the entrance. This clerk was young, barely more than a boy, with blond hair and a freckled face. He smiled at Evergrow. The walnut-coloured coat that he wore was shorter than those worn by the clerks at the desk, in keeping with his juniority, and his job was to go on errands in the Butlery for the more senior clerks. But an errand such as this – taking a message to the Butler that a Halibut had come to see him – wasn't something for a beginner, and the junior clerk had been left waiting for another errand to run.

But it seemed to be a very quiet morning. No one else came in. Ten minutes passed, according to the big clock above the desk. Then another ten. Evergrow glanced at the junior clerk again, who smiled back at him and gave a slight shrug, as if to say a wait like this was only to be expected. Meanwhile, the clerk at the desk scratched at his account book with his pen, glancing up from time to time to check something from another account book in front of him.

'Excuse me,' said Evergrow at last to the clerk behind the desk. 'Can you tell me what's happening?'

'You're waiting,' he muttered, without taking his eyes off his work.

'For what?'

'For Mr Fellowes to come back.'

'Where's he gone?'

'Lunch.' The clerk glanced over his shoulder at the clock. 'Oh,' he said sarcastically, 'it's only ten o'clock. Maybe he's gone to find the Butler and ask him about your case.'

'I don't have a case,' said Evergrow.

'Oh, yes, you do, sir. You have a very peculiar case, if you don't mind my saying so. It's the case of a boy who turns up with information concerning an individual who is the subject of quite considerable interest, yet refuses to divulge it to two Clerks of the Entrance – *two* Clerks of the Entrance, I repeat, not merely one – including the estimable Mr Fellowes and, of course, Mr Childes, whose qualities are not for me to comment on, since I am, in fact, he.'

'I don't know what you're talking about,' said Evergrow.

'Your case, Evergrow D Halibut.'

'But I don't have a case.'

'You do now. I've just been recording it.' Childes held up his account book. 'Here it is, in black and white.' He turned over one page after another. 'What greater proof can you ask for?'

'Well, I don't think it's such a peculiar case,' remarked Evergrow.

'That's not for you to judge,' replied the clerk severely, and he turned back to his writing with a look of intense concentration on his face, as if the case, with Evergrow's last remark, had grown even more peculiar. 'Others will judge that for you.'

Evergrow frowned. He glanced at the junior clerk, who had listened to the conversation with interest, and now gave one of his sympathetic shrugs. But this wasn't exactly the reception Evergrow had expected. The clerks of the Butlery were there to look after the business of the Halibuts, he had always thought. That wasn't how it felt. It felt as if he was intruding in a place that had nothing at all to do with him, where the clerks who sat behind the desk, at least, would have been much happier if he and every other Halibut didn't exist.

He watched the clock. It was an instrument of ancient construction, with a big white face from which hung a complicated set of weights and pulleys, one or other of which would twitch or jerk from time to time.

The waiting seemed to go on forever. The senior clerk wrote. The junior clerk watched. Each time Evergrow was about to speak again, the senior clerk would glance up, as if anticipating, and the look in his eyes seemed to say that Evergrow's case would only grow more peculiar, and the delay in the return of the other clerk even longer, if he said anything else.

Finally the door behind the desk opened and Fellowes returned. He didn't say anything to Evergrow, but went immediately to the other clerk and looked at his account book. He turned page after page, reading carefully. Finally he nodded and looked up at Evergrow.

'The Butler will see you now,' he announced.

Evergrow stared at him in surprise. He opened his mouth to reply, but Fellowes interrupted him before he could speak.

'I warn you, your case is peculiar.'

'I warned him already,' said Childes.

'Remember that before you speak, Evergrow D Halibut. It's not my place to give you advice, but I would advise you that anything you say, in my opinion, can only add to its peculiarity. Now, what you do with that advice is up to you, although I should warn you that anything you do do with it may well add even more to the peculiarity of your case. In fact, it's almost guaranteed to.'

The other clerk nodded seriously, his pen poised to write, and only waiting, it seemed, for Evergrow to do something.

Evergrow stood up. He hesitated for a moment, watching the two clerks, who returned his gaze with eager, almost predatory expressions.

'Did you say the Butler would see me?' he said.

'Nothing wrong with the memory,' muttered Fellowes to Childes, who made a note.

'Where is he?' asked Evergrow.

'Wouldn't you like to know?'

'Well . . . yes. You said he wants to see me, didn't you?'

'No need to labour the point,' replied Fellowes irritably. 'Let's go.'

Evergrow started to go around the desk to the door the clerk had used.

'*Not that door!*' cried Fellowes, and Childes jumped up as if to protect it with his body. 'That's the clerk's door, sir. Are you a clerk, sir? Is that what you are, sir? A clerk, sir?'

'No,' said Evergrow.

'Then can you explain what possible reason you might have to use the clerk's door?'

'No,' said Evergrow.

'No,' said Fellowes, 'I didn't think you could.' He threw back his head, cleared his throat, ran his fingers through his whiskers and straightened the lapels of his walnut-coloured coat, which had become somewhat rumpled in the excitement.

Childes did exactly the same thing, with the exception of smoothing his whiskers, which he lacked. He threw a mistrustful glance at Evergrow and sat down again.

'*That* door,' said Fellowes, pointing to yet another door that led from the room.

Evergrow glanced at it doubtfully.

'That's it, sir. Out you go!' Fellowes waved a hand disdainfully in its direction.

Evergrow gave the young freckled clerk a last glance, opened the door and went out. He found himself in a corridor. A moment later, Fellowes appeared around a corner.

'Follow me,' he said, and marched quickly away, without once glancing back to make sure Evergrow was keeping up.

They passed room after room, and through doorway after doorway Evergrow saw clerk after clerk at work behind desks overflowing with papers and files, with shelfloads of more papers and files on the walls around them. They went up stairs, around corners, down stairs and around more corners, and still the rooms kept coming, with desk after desk of clerks hard at work. No piece of business within Neversuch House was not checked, double-checked and then filed forever within the archives of the Butlery. Every item purchased or hired from the outside world, every item kept, consumed, broken or returned, was noted and recorded. Somewhere deep within this vast honeycomb of rooms were the records dating back to the First Captain himself, including the records of the building of the House, the materials purchased, the workers hired, the wages paid, the food provided, the expenses reimbursed. On one particularly dusty shelf high up in one particularly dusty room there was even a book listing the costs for the graves dug for those workers who had fallen from a roof or a turret under construction, which ran to several hundred pages.

And at the centre of all this sat the Hereditary Butler, Digby.

At last, the clerk stopped. He knocked twice at a red door, waited, gave Evergrow a last, mistrustful look, then opened the door and stood back. 'In you go,' he hissed, and he pushed Evergrow forward before closing the door behind him.

An enormous desk stood in the room, covered with a jumble of in-trays and out-trays piled high with files. All around the room were metal safes and big chests of drawers with padlocks. On the walls hung paintings of the past Hereditary Butlers, all sitting at this same desk in this same room behind a very similar-looking jumble of files, going all the way back to the first Butler, the original Digby. All the men in the paintings were small men with brown eyes, as had been the first of the Digbys on the wall, as was the latest Digby who now occupied the chair behind the desk.

His head poked out from among the in-trays and out-trays in front of him.

'You took your time getting here,' said the Butler. 'I've been waiting for you for over an hour.'

'But I was waiting at the entrance,' said Evergrow. 'They didn't bring me until now.'

Digby looked at him suspiciously, craning his head around an in-tray to get a better look. Then he sighed. Although he had become Hereditary Butler on the death of his father, he had the feeling that the clerks were running everything, and he didn't know what they were telling him and what they weren't. If it wasn't for Tobias Hildegrew, he felt, he would have been utterly lost.

'They told me my case was peculiar,' said Evergrow. 'I thought maybe that's why it was taking so long.'

'What case is that?' asked Digby.

'Didn't they tell you?'

Digby shook his head.

Evergrow frowned. 'I thought you'd know.'

'You'd better tell me before—'

The door opened. In marched the three UnderButlers, Trimbleby, Withers and Dish.

'Too late,' sighed Digby.

The UnderButlers were all big men, almost bursting out of their prune-coloured coats. Trimbleby had a huge, purplish nose that was pitted like a pickle. Withers had half a dozen strands of hair carefully plastered across a scalp that would otherwise have been entirely bald. And Dish had a small chin flanked by a pair of drooping cheeks that made him look somewhat like a basset hound.

Now that the old Butler was gone, each was trying to make sure he would become the most important UnderButler for the new one. Consequently, instead of doing their work, they were spending most of their time in the Butler's office or spying on each other to make sure that no one got to spend time with the Butler unless they were there as well.

'Carry on!' said Trimbleby loudly. He was naturally a loud man and his strategy was to be even louder than ever, trying to take control of everything and hoping in this way to impress the Butler.

'If Mr Digby agrees,' said Withers, whose approach, in accordance with his nature, was to defer constantly to the Butler, hoping that would win his favour.

The approach taken by Dish, a quieter type, was different again. He put his nose in the air, stroked his drooping cheeks, and remained silent, as if to say, 'While these other two are just trying to impress you, *I'm* the one you should trust.'

Digby sighed again. He would have liked to get rid of the UnderButlers and send them off to work somewhere else in the Butlery, but he had no idea how anything in the Butlery actually operated and he was too frightened to risk it. Tobias Hildegrew seemed to know how to stand up to them in a way that Digby himself couldn't. The Butler wished that Tobias was here now. But Tobias was probably off doing something useful, which was more than could be said for the three UnderButlers.

He turned back wearily to Evergrow. 'What is it you wanted to tell me?'

'I have a message from Omnia Halibut,' replied Evergrow. 'She's in hiding and—'

'Where?' demanded Trimbleby immediately. 'Where is she?'

'Please be quiet, Mr Trimbleby' said Digby. 'Let the boy speak.'

'Exactly,' murmured Withers. 'I would never have interrupted like that.'

Dish shuffled meaningfully on the spot, desperately

trying to attract Digby's attention so the Butler would notice that he had stayed silent.

'Go on,' said Digby to Evergrow.

'Nothing that's been said about her is true. She hasn't been outside the wall.'

'Nonsense!' retorted Trimbleby. 'She was seen there.'

'She wasn't. That's a lie. I have a message from her.' Evergrow turned to the Butler. 'Omnia knows who killed your father.'

There was a gasp and suddenly all three of the Under-Butlers were shouting. '*Killed him?*' '*No!*' '*How?*' '*Never!*' '*When?*'

'Please . . .' groaned Digby.

Evergrow watched them in amazement. Basilica had said the UnderButlers would have their own suspicions about the Butler's so-called accident. It didn't look like it.

'What are you talking about?' demanded Trimbleby, his booming voice overpowering the others. 'Killed him? Whoever heard such nonsense?'

'Omnia has proof. She knows who did it.'

'Who?'

'She wouldn't tell me.'

'She'll tell me!' bellowed Trimbleby.

'No, she won't. She'll only tell the Butler.'

Trimbleby snorted. Withers shook his head. And Dish furiously stroked his cheeks.

In the mean time, the door had opened. Tobias Hildegrew came in.

'Thank goodness,' murmured Digby in relief.

'Yes, just as you'd expect, here he is when he isn't needed,' muttered Trimbleby snidely, and Withers and Dish glared at him. If there was one thing that was guaranteed to unite the three UnderButlers, it was their jealousy of Tobias Hildegrew.

'Go away!' said Trimbleby. 'This is official business.'

'Yes, go on, get out!' said Withers.

'What's going on?' asked Hildegrew, entirely ignoring them. He stood near the Butler. 'It's Evergrow, isn't it?'

Evergrow nodded.

'He says my father was killed,' said Digby, 'and Omnia Halibut knows who did it.'

'Preposterous!' snapped Trimbleby.

The Butler sighed. 'Mr Trimbleby, don't you think we should at least hear—'

'No, Mr Digby, I don't. And as for all this talk of your father being killed, I don't think this is something we should be talking about in front of . . .' Trimbleby stopped and waved a hand in Evergrow's direction.

'Who?' said Tobias Hildegrew.

'Who do you *think*?' snapped the UnderButler.

'It's obvious,' muttered Withers, and Dish nodded gravely.

'Omnia has proof,' said Evergrow.

'Does she?' said Tobias Hildegrew. 'Where is she?'

'In hiding,' muttered Withers sarcastically.

'She was never outside the wall,' said Evergrow. 'That's a lie.'

'Is it?' demanded Trimbleby. 'And I suppose she has proof of that as well, does she?'

Tobias Hildegrew turned to Digby. 'If there's even a chance your father was killed, perhaps I should—'

'Don't *talk* like that in front of the *boy*!' hissed Trimbleby.

'It's not as if we haven't thought of it,' said Withers. 'We've taken precautions.'

'We'd take even more,' said Dish, throwing a resentful glance in Hildegrew's direction, 'if a certain person would stop objecting.'

Evergrow watched them. He was starting to see what was going on. The UnderButlers did have their suspicions, but didn't want to show their concerns in front of him. Or in front of any Halibut, probably.

'Perhaps I should go and hear what she has to say,' said Hildegrew to Digby once the UnderButlers had finished.

'Oh, we should hear what she has to say all right,' said Trimbleby. He turned to Evergrow. 'Take us to her!'

'I don't know where she is. I've brought a message, that's all.'

'You're lying, boy! You do know where she is. Do you know what we do to lying Halibuts?'

'Mr Trimbleby . . .' said Digby.

'Do you?' demanded Trimbleby again, and he came closer to Evergrow and bent down, putting his huge pickle of a nose in Evergrow's face. 'Do you know what we do?'

'Mr Trimbleby . . .' said Digby again.

Trimbleby narrowed his eyes, gazed menacingly at

Evergrow for another moment and then slowly straightened up.

'Evergrow,' said Tobias Hildegrew. 'Is that true? You don't know where she is?'

'All I have is a message. All I can tell you is what she wants to do.'

'And what's that?'

'She's prepared to meet Mr Digby to tell him who killed his father.'

'Why hasn't she come now?' asked Digby

'Because . . .' Evergrow hesitated, wondering how much he should say. 'Because people are looking for her. If they find her before she gets here, they'll get her.'

'And bring her here,' said Withers. 'What's the problem?'

Evergrow hesitated again. 'It has to be at night. That's the other thing.'

'Why?'

'It has to be. That's what she said. I can't change it. I'm not going to see her again. I'm just here to tell you what she said. Tomorrow night, at midnight, in the Silent Cloister.'

'Ridiculous!' scoffed Trimbleby. 'Everything you've said is ridiculous from start to finish. You don't fool me, boy! You're not going to see her again? Of course you're going to see her again. And when you do, you can tell her to forget it. She can come here herself or she can stay in hiding forever. Tell her *that* and see how she likes it!'

Evergrow stared at Trimbleby in alarm. He had no idea

209

what Omnia would do if that was the answer he was going to have to take back to her.

'You can stop pretending you don't know where she is, young man. Go straight back there and tell her what I said.'

'Who does she want to meet?' asked Tobias Hildegrew.

Evergrow turned to him quickly. 'Just Mr Digby. And she says the UnderButlers should come as well.'

Trimbleby snorted.

Hildegrew glanced at the Butler. 'I don't see why not. If that's how she wants to do it.'

'At midnight in the Silent Cloister?'

Hildegrew smiled. 'A bit dramatic, perhaps, but I don't see what difference it makes. If she wants to do it like that, we can let her have her fun.'

'We're not here for her to have fun!' snapped Trimbleby.

Hildegrew ignored him. 'Tell us exactly how she wants to do it, Evergrow.'

'Mr Digby and the UnderButlers are to be in the Silent Cloister tomorrow night. They should hide themselves so no one can see them. At midnight, Omnia will come.'

'And in the mean time, can we do anything to help her?'

Evergrow shook his head. 'Just don't tell anyone else. If she sees anyone else in the Cloister before she gets there, she's going to turn around and leave. You won't even see her.'

'Won't we just?' said Withers. 'And how she's going to get there? Is she going to fly there on the big black bird?'

Dish grinned.

The Butler glanced at Tobias Hildegrew.

'I don't see why not,' said Tobias again.

'I do!' snapped Trimbleby. 'She's the last person who should be setting conditions! Mr Digby, you should tell this boy to tell Omnia Halibut to come here at once!'

There was silence. Everyone's eyes were on the Butler.

The Butler glanced at Tobias once more. Hildegrew nodded slightly.

'I'll be there,' said the Butler. 'And the UnderButlers too.'

The UnderButlers stared at him, fuming.

'If you do happen to see her, Evergrow, tell Omnia we'll do exactly what she said.'

In the room at the entrance, the two clerks at the desk glared at Evergrow when he reappeared, but they didn't dare say a word, seeing that Tobias Hildegrew was with him. The junior clerk was still sitting beside the door and gave Evergrow a last smile as he left.

Evergrow went down. But his job wasn't finished. He still had to find Cornelius Slinker. Only then would the trap be set.

He didn't have long to look. Slinker found him. Almost as soon as Evergrow had crossed the court in front of the Bright Tower, he heard someone whisper his name. He looked around. From behind a column beckoned a dark figure.

Cornelius Slinker pulled the hood of his messenger's

cloak back from his head. 'Saw you go in,' he muttered. 'Waited for you.'

'Have you been following me?'

'Where's Omnia?'

'How should I know?'

Slinker gazed at him with his deep-set eyes. 'Take me to her.'

'I told you, I don't know where she is.'

'She needs protection.'

'And I suppose you'll give it to her, will you?' said Evergrow. 'I suppose that's why you followed us yesterday. I suppose that's why you ran after us, is it?'

The messenger nodded. 'Take me to her. She needs help.'

Evergrow could just imagine what kind of help Cornelius Slinker had in mind. 'You want to see her, do you?'

Slinker nodded quickly.

'Then I'll tell you a secret. She'll be in the Silent Cloister tomorrow at midnight. But don't tell anyone else or she won't come.'

Slinker shook his head. 'I can't wait for tomorrow. She's in too much danger.'

'Bad luck. Tomorrow night, no earlier. Don't tell anyone else. If you want to see her, be there.'

Slinker grabbed his arm. 'Take me to her now!'

Evergrow pulled his arm loose. 'Tomorrow at midnight! That's your only chance.' He took a couple of steps back. 'And don't try to follow me! If you follow me, she won't come at all.'

212

Evergrow ran off. He had done everything Omnia had asked. That night, he would go back to the hiding place in the Ribbled Lodge to bring food and tell her that everything was ready for her plan. He had his own plan as well – but he had no intention of letting Omnia know about that.

He stopped at the archway that led to the steps beside the Bright Tower and looked back to make sure Slinker wasn't following. Then he went down the stairs.

As he did, he didn't think to look up and see who might be watching him from the windows in the Bright Tower above.

20

Night Terror

Omnia awoke in a sweat. She had had the dream. It wasn't the first time. She had had it the night before, and the night before that.

In the dream she was falling from the Slate Tower. She was plummeting into the terror of thin air and the black cloak was fluttering above her and she knew someone was watching her fall, somehow she *knew* it, and it was the person who had thrown her off the Tower but she couldn't see him because of the cloak. Suddenly the cloak turned into the great black bird and flew away. Now she could see the person looking down at her, but as hard as she looked, she couldn't make out the features of his face, but she knew that if only she could see his features this terrible fall would stop and she would be saved. As the dream went on, she kept falling, falling, staring at him, desperately trying to see who it was, but the face was a smooth, sheer blank and the harder she looked the less she could see and the more desperate and terrified she became.

Normally the dream continued until an instant before she hit the ground and she awoke in cold terror, with that same feeling of icy fear she had felt when she had really been thrown off the Tower. But this time she woke earlier, while she was still falling and trying to see the face.

She lay in the darkness, trying to drive the terror away. Then she heard something. Suddenly she remembered where she was. Now she understood why she had woken earlier in the dream than usual. A noise had disturbed her. She heard it again. Footsteps. Somewhere above her head. On the roof. Not far away.

The footsteps stopped. There was silence for a few seconds. Then they started up again, and then there was silence. The cycle repeated. *Footsteps, silence . . . Footsteps, silence . . .*

Omnia listened in the darkness, trying to work out what was happening above her on the roof of the Ribbled Lodge. Had Evergrow forgotten which chimney led to the hiding place? But why was he here again? He had already been there earlier that night to bring food and tell her that he had seen the Butler and Cornelius Slinker. Why was he back now?

Footsteps, silence . . . Footsteps, silence . . .

Suddenly Omnia knew what was happening. Someone was checking the chimneys, going from one to the next. And it wasn't Evergrow.

She sat up. Her heart pounded. She didn't dare light the

lantern. She listened for a moment longer, then noiselessly got to her feet. She went to the window.

As quietly and gently as she could, she inched the window open. It squeaked.

The footsteps stopped.

Omnia hardly dared to breathe. She stared into the darkness, frowning listening.

Footsteps.

A shaft of light poked down the chimney into the room.

Omnia slammed her hand against the window and almost hurled herself over the sill and out into the night, scrabbling with her feet for the first of the footholds that were supposedly beneath her. Down she went. Down down down, not even thinking of the drop that awaited her should she fumble. She heard the thud of someone landing in the room she had just left. She went even faster, if that was possible. She heard a hissing from the window above her. But she didn't look up. Something whistled past in the darkness. Something else came plummeting out of the window, her own lantern, and crashed into her arm. It knocked one of her hands loose and she swung for an instant and then fell. But the ground was just below her and she landed with a jolt and was up and running before she even felt the pain of the impact. She got to the corner of the Lodge and looked around to see a black figure coming out of the window, its cloak flapping at its arms.

She ran. Under an arch that led to the Pastel Court, then left, then right, seeking corners, turns, anything that would put a pursuer in doubt behind her. Across the Potted Terrace, up the stairs to the Short Promenade, left, right at the end, right again, down some stairs, left, right, right, losing all sense of where she was now, left, left, right, left, and then she found herself at the Splitted Stairs. Five arms of the staircase to choose from. She saw an empty niche, dark, of the kind where a statue might have stood, where no moonlight fell. She climbed up and pressed back into the darkness.

Her heart raced. For a couple of minutes she could hear nothing but the blood surging in her ears.

Eventually her breathing slowed. The pounding in her ears diminished. She looked around her in the niche. A face! She almost jumped out. But it was carved into the stone at the back of the niche, a grimacing, leering face, one of the little jokes the first Captain's masons had left when they built the house.

She listened again. Her senses were at the utmost limit of alertness – sight, hearing, touch – she was like some kind of wind-up toy with a spring, ready to jump and run.

She heard footsteps. Run? Or stay? She shrank back into the shadow of the niche, her head, her back, her legs, every part of her body pressed to the wall behind her as if she could somehow make it meld into the surface. The same footsteps? She couldn't tell. They came closer. They stopped. Still she couldn't see anyone. They started up again and moved away.

Whose footsteps had it been? Was it *him*?

If it was, he might be waiting somewhere, hoping that she would think she was safe and come out. She stayed where she was, pressed deep into the shadow.

The silence continued. Omnia looked up. She could see the face of a clock in the Narrow Tower, pale in the moonlight. It was almost two in the morning. Now there were footsteps again. Omnia shrank back. These ones kept coming. Eventually a big man in a dressing gown waddled past and went up the third arm of the Splitted Steps, not noticing Omnia or even throwing a glance at the niche in which she was hiding.

Omnia hadn't seen his face. It could have been Everfull Halibut, or possibly Everround, Eversmart's father, who was nearly as large. Where was he going at two in the morning?

Silence. Omnia began to feel slightly safer. Perhaps she really had managed to get away.

She became aware of a sound. It was a voice singing. Omnia looked up and saw a woman in a window high above her. The window could have been in the Bartled Range or the Storied Stack, both of which rose high in this part of the House. In the darkness, Omnia couldn't be sure. The song sounded like something out of an opera. The woman moved her arms theatrically as she sang and then threw her head back, eyes closed, her mouth wide in a crescendo of sound.

Omnia stared in amazement. Kyrelia Halibut! Kyrelia Halibut, always as quiet as a mouse and dressed like a mouse as well. Not now. Her black hair, normally gathered up

218

tight in a bun, hung free down her back in long, gleaming locks. Instead of her usual plain, dark dress she wore a shimmering green gown. Her voice was beautiful, sweet. It seemed to Omnia that the night had turned drab Kyrelia into a kind of glittering songbird.

There were lights in other windows as well, like holes in a huge, black canvas. Not far from Kyrelia, above her and to the left, someone was facing out into the night with a smile on his face, perhaps listening to her voice and wondering who was singing, unable to see her. It looked like Eversniff T Halibut, who was always so grumpy.

In another window, lower down, sat Pyrelia Halibut and Posteria Halibut, deep in discussion. Omnia had never seen them exchange a single word and everyone knew that they had had a fight as girls, over fifty years before, and had never made it up. And elsewhere, someone was working at something, maybe a shoe, wearing a dirty old leather apron and hunched over the object with a metal tool that flashed in the light. It looked like Everclip N Halibut, the most fastidious man in the House, who wouldn't even touch an apple unless he had personally seen it being washed and cleaned of every last speck of dirt. And here he was, wearing an old apron and bashing away with a set of tools!

Kyrelia's singing went on. Omnia listened. It seemed to her that what she could see from the niche was another, magical world in the House, some kind of reverse existence that came to life only at night.

She looked back at the clock in the tower. It was

after three now. Where had the time gone? Surely she hadn't been listening to the singing for so long. It felt like minutes. Omnia poked her head out of the niche and looked cautiously from side to side. She got down. And as she did, it seemed that Kyrelia's singing came to an end, and when she glanced over her shoulder at where Kyrelia and the others had been, there was nothing but darkness.

Omnia took the fourth arm of the Splitted Stairs. It brought her out behind the Hall of Leaning.

A faint glow came from the windows of the Hall.

Omnia slipped along the side of the building and quietly opened the door. She peered around the corner of the first bookcase. All alone in the hall at one of the desks sat Pedagogia Halibut, the unofficial headmistress and poet, studying a book under a lamp. For a minute or so Omnia watched her. She was reminded of the things Basilica had said. Nothing in the House was as it seemed. Still Pedagogia read, unaware that anyone else was present. Omnia slipped quickly across the sloping floor.

'Hello,' she said.

Pedagogia looked up with a start.

'Don't call out!' said Omnia fiercely. 'You'll be sorry if you do!'

Pedagogia nodded quickly. Omnia could see real fear in the headmistress's eyes. Omnia wondered what people had been saying about her, what they were telling each other she had done when she went outside the wall.

'You shouldn't believe everything you hear,' said Omnia darkly.

Pedagogia frowned. 'Are you all right, Omnia? We've all been worried.'

'I'm all right.'

'Omnia . . .' Pedagogia hesitated for a moment. 'Why did you go outside the wall?'

'I didn't go outside the wall.'

'It's a very serious thing that you've done.' Pedagogia sighed. 'It's only worse if you deny it. Tell the truth and—'

'I am telling the truth! Anyway, I didn't come here to talk about that. It's not *me* telling the truth that's the question.' Omnia pulled a chair across from another desk and sat down. She gazed intently into Pedagogia's eyes. 'Why are we being told lies?'

Pedagogia sat back sharply. 'Who's telling you lies?'

'You are,' said Omnia. 'Everyone is.'

'I'm sorry, Omnia, but that simply isn't true.'

'It is true!'

'I don't know where you get that idea. I don't know how you dare to—'

'From Basilica.'

At the mention of the name, a look of utter amazement came across Pedagogia's face. 'Basilica Halibut? Is that who you mean? Basilica Halibut?'

Omnia nodded.

'You've spoken to her? You've seen her? You couldn't have!'

'Well, I did.'

221

'She's dead.'

Now it was Omnia's turn to stare in surprise.

'Where did you see her?'

'Somewhere.'

'Here?' said Pedagogia. 'In the House? I don't believe you. You *have* been outside the wall!'

'I haven't!'

'Then where is she?'

'Somewhere in the House. I'm not going to tell you where.' Omnia paused. She wasn't supposed to tell anyone about Basilica at all. 'If you tell anyone I saw her, I'll deny I ever said it!'

Pedagogia gazed at her, as if trying to decide whether Omnia might be telling the truth. 'What did she tell you?' she asked at last.

'She said that nothing about Neversuch House is as it seems.'

Pedagogia watched her for a moment longer. Then she laughed. 'Well, that certainly sounds like her. Typical Basilica! Just what I'd expect. You could never believe a word she said.'

'Are you saying it isn't true?'

'Look around you, Omnia. Look at these books. Thousands of them. Are you saying none of them is true? Are you saying all the knowledge, the learning, the wisdom, the facts, the evidence, the observations, the logic, the conclusions – everything they contain – are you saying all of that is false?'

Omnia didn't mean it exactly like that.

'Then how can Basilica be right?' demanded Pedagogia.

'Maybe it's not what's in the books, but what isn't.'

'Is that what she said? Omnia, what you have to under-stand about Basilica is that she was . . .' Pedagogia stopped, shaking her head.

'What?' said Omnia.

'Nothing.' Pedagogia paused. 'No one could ever under-stand Basilica. And how can you trust someone you don't understand? Well, Omnia? How can you trust someone like that?'

Omnia thought about it. She didn't understand Basilica, that was certainly true. In fact, Basilica was easily the least understandable person she had ever met, which made her all the more interesting. But whether you couldn't trust someone just because you couldn't understand her, Omnia wasn't at all sure whether that was right.

'How can you ever know when she's telling the truth?'

'Why don't *you* tell the truth?' demanded Omnia. 'When was the last time you saw her?'

'What's that got to do with it?'

'Why didn't you know she was here in the House? Why didn't you even know she was alive?'

'I'm sorry, I refuse to take part in this conversation.'

'Exactly!'

'Let me warn you, Omnia, for your own sake. Some things never change. If Basilica's really alive, then trust her if you dare. But be warned. Basilica's bad. She doesn't know herself when she's telling the truth and when she's telling lies.'

Omnia was silent. How was it that the murderer had found her hiding place in the roof of the Ribbled Lodge? Only Basilica and Evergrow knew she was there. But if Basilica had told the killer, why had he waited for the second night to come after her? How could he even know she would still be there on the second night? And why hadn't he known which chimney to look in? Perhaps he had forgotten. Perhaps he had become confused in the darkness. Perhaps all of this, this whole strange plot in which she seemed to be entangled, was being orchestrated by Basilica herself from the Slate Tower.

Pedagogia was watching her. 'Well, Omnia. I'm right, aren't I? You can't trust her. She lies and lies. That's all she ever did.'

Omnia frowned. It seemed to her that Pedagogia really hated Basilica. Something must have happened between them. Long ago, something which could still put so much feeling into Pedagogia's words.

'Believe me, all of this that Basilica's told you, it's just nonsense. Evil nonsense. Don't believe a word of it.'

Was it nonsense, as the headmistress said? Suddenly Omnia knew how to test her. 'Basilica told me about the Evergones.'

A ripple of dismay crossed Pedagogia's face, too quick and too instinctive for her to hide.

'What did she tell you?'

Omnia smiled.

'What?'

'I'm not saying.'

'Well . . .' Pedagogia forced a laugh. 'Whatever she said, it's nonsense again. It's just Basilica with her lies. Evergones? What are they? There are no such things. They're a myth. Fairy stories.'

Omnia watched Pedagogia knowingly. The headmistress could say what she liked. The look on her face had spoken more loudly, and more clearly, than any number of words. The Evergones weren't nonsense. And if they weren't, why should anything else Basilica had told her be nonsense either?

'You can't trust her, Omnia! Believe me, you can't trust a word she says. She was always like that, even as a girl.'

Omnia got up.

'Where are you going?'

'Don't try to follow me! You'll be sorry if you do.'

'Omnia, listen. Whatever you've done, tell the truth about it. Why did you go outside the wall? Who made you do it? Was it Basilica?'

'I didn't go outside the wall.'

'It was Basilica, wasn't it? I should have known. Just like her. She'll use you, Omnia, don't think that she won't.'

'She's not *using* me.'

'She's still hatching her schemes, isn't she? Up to her tricks again. She never changes. If only you knew what she'd done! What's she making you do?'

'Nothing!'

'Where is she, Omnia? Tell me! Where did you see her?'

Pedagogia reached for Omnia's arm. Omnia jumped back, knocking over her chair. It slid away on the sloping floor.

'Omnia. Please. Tell me what happened.'

'Who's Basilica to you? How do you know about her? What happened to her? *What?*'

Pedagogia didn't speak.

'You knew her when you were younger, didn't you? Was she your friend? What happened between you? Why do you hate her so much? Tell me why you didn't know she's here! Tell me why you didn't even know she's alive!'

Pedagogia didn't speak. She gazed at Omnia, lips tightly closed.

'You're too scared to say.'

'She's using you, Omnia. I'm warning you. Don't be fooled. Whatever she's telling you to do, it's only so she can use you for her own evil schemes.'

Omnia gazed at Pedagogia. Then she shook her head. 'You're just trying to turn me against her.' Omnia went halfway to the door of the Hall. 'I'm warning you, don't follow me. Don't even try.' Omnia got to the door, glanced back at Pedagogia and then slipped out.

She ran across to the shadow under the overhanging roof of the Low Gallery and hugged the wall. Then she stopped in the darkness of a doorway, wondering where to go next.

In front of her rose the Great Tower. The moon was

226

high behind it. Suddenly it seemed to Omnia that she saw the great black bird rise and glide across the moon. But if she really had seen it – if it even existed – within a moment it was gone, lost in the darkness.

She stood in the doorway, trying to decide what to do next. Her hiding place in the Ribbled Lodge had been discovered. She couldn't go back there. Yet there was still one day to go until her appointment in the Silent Cloister.

One more day, she thought to herself. If only she could survive it.

She stood a moment longer, then stepped out of the doorway and ran.

21

The Last Day

The ivy brushed at Omnia's face. She tapped at the glass.

Nothing.

She tapped again, and again, dreading to see someone peering at her from another window.

Then Evergrow was there in his blue flannel pyjamas. He blinked. His eyes went wide when he saw her.

Omnia tumbled inside. She told him what had happened, or at least about her escape from the Ribbled Lodge. She didn't tell him that she had found Pedagogia in the Hall of Leaning or what the headmistress had to say about Basilica. Evergrow had enough doubts about Basilica already.

'So you think it was Basilica who gave you away?' said Evergrow, exactly as Omnia expected.

'It could have been someone else.'

'Who?'

'You.'

'Is that what you think?' demanded Evergrow.

'No. Keep your voice down. Of course I don't think you gave me away. I wouldn't have come here if I didn't trust you, would I?'

'Then why did you say that?' asked Evergrow. He looked really hurt.

'Evergrow, if it wasn't Basilica, it must have been you. I mean, not on purpose, but you must have been followed. How else can you explain it?'

'Why would anyone follow me?'

Omnia stared at him. Wasn't it obvious? Twice already Cornelius Slinker had tried to get Evergrow to take him to her.

'Omnia, I swear I didn't know he was following me. I swear I didn't. I kept looking around. I kept checking behind me.'

Omnia nodded. It would be hard to make sure you weren't followed, especially at night. And especially by someone like Cornelius Slinker. 'At least he didn't know which chimney it was. That would have been the end of me.'

She closed her eyes, reliving those moments when she awoke in the dark from her terrifying dream to the even more terrifying sound of the footsteps walking over the roof above her. She shivered.

'Omnia, do you think he'll come here?'

'It's possible.'

Evergrow jumped up and went to look out the window.

'Get down,' said Omnia. 'If he's watching, he'll guess something's going on.'

'Do you think he is?'

Omnia shook her head. It was too obvious. If Slinker had followed Evergrow to the Ribbled Lodge, the last place he would expect Omnia to go would be back to Evergrow's apartment. That was the reason she had come here. That and the fact she didn't really have anywhere else to hide.

'Make sure your door's locked,' she said.

Evergrow got up and locked his door. He came back to her. 'Omnia, you can't go ahead with this by yourself. It's too dangerous.'

'The Butler and the UnderButlers will be there. He won't do anything to me in front of them.'

'What if he gets to you before that? He knows you're coming to the Silent Cloister. What if he gets you on the way in?'

'I've thought of that.'

'Why don't you let me—'

'I've got it all worked out.'

'Omnia, you can't go alone!'

'Keep your voice down.'

'You *can't*!'

Omnia shrugged.

'You're just being stubborn.'

'I'm not being stubborn.'

'You are. You're the most stubborn person I know.'

'Me? Stubborn?' Omnia stared at him in disbelief. 'When? When have I *ever* been stubborn?'

Evergrow stared at her in even greater disbelief. 'Omnia Halibut, are you serious? When have you ever *not* been stubborn? Listen to me. You cannot go by yourself.'

'And what are you going to do about it?'

Evergrow opened his mouth to reply, but then thought better of it.

'Well?' Omnia gazed at him.

Evergrow looked away, biting his lip.

'Come on, Evergrow,' said Omnia, forcing a smile. She felt bad for having said that to him. After everything he had done for her, he didn't deserve that. 'I'll be all right. Don't worry about me.'

Evergrow nodded, still not looking at her.

'I will. You'll see. I'll come back from there all right.'

'Alive, you mean?' said Evergrow.

'Yes,' she said. Omnia paused for a moment. 'Alive.'

She slept in Evergrow's wardrobe and woke late, having been up for so much of the night. She came out cautiously into his bedroom, which was bright with sunlight. Evergrow was gone, but had already brought back breakfast for her, toast and jam and a couple of blueberry muffins. She ate hungrily.

Later, she went through the back of the wardrobe into the room she had discovered the last time she was here. It was just as she had first found it, the dust, the cobwebs, the crockery and the skeleton of the bird lying in its cage. And the paintings. She looked at them. They *were* of Basilica, she was sure of it. She examined the one of Basilica with the man. Who was he? The brother Basilica had mentioned? They were smiling when it was painted. They were happy.

Try as she might, Omnia couldn't drive Pedagogia's words completely out of her head. What had Basilica done in the past? *Was* Basilica using her? Had she become a pawn in a game that she didn't even understand?

Omnia looked around the room. Everything remained just as it had been the first time she came in here. The wax hung from the candlestick like two frozen waterfalls. The small, frail skeleton of the bird still lay on the floor of the birdcage, where it had been left to rot. The plate and cutlery and wine glass and jug were scattered across the table, as if a meal had been interrupted.

She walked to the end of the room. In the corner, where the light was at its dimmest, she found a small door which she hadn't noticed before. She opened it. Inside was a tiny annex with a toilet and a tap. Just as there had been in the room under the roof of the Ribbled Lodge . . .

Suddenly Omnia knew what had happened here. Someone had been chased out, just as she had been from the Ribbled Lodge. If you went back to the room in the Ribbled Lodge, you'd find the blankets she had slept on and the food she hadn't eaten and the bag she had carried and everything else she had left behind in her panicked scramble to get away from Cornelius Slinker. And if you went back there in twenty years, unless someone else had been there first, you'd find the same things, only the food might have rotted away and left a blackened crust.

The same thing had happened here. Someone had left behind their meal and the burning candles and the bird, and whoever had then sealed the room off had left the bird to die, out of sheer cruelty, perhaps, or out of frustration.

She glanced at the windows. They would have been open on the day the person who had last sat here had made his escape, not yet concealed behind unpruned ivy. She knew how he would have got out. Through a window and down the ivy he had climbed with not a moment to take anything with him.

Or *her*. Was it Basilica who had been here? Was *she* the one who had made the escape?

Omnia looked around, but there was no clue. She turned to the chest of drawers. Basilica had asked about it so it must be important. Last time she had tried to open the drawers but hadn't succeeded. She tried again. She pulled hard on the top one. Then the second. There was a tiny bit of movement. She pulled and pulled. Suddenly the drawer opened with a screech. It was a huge drawer but contained only a couple of old shirts. Omnia held them up. Big. A man's shirts, probably. Insects had nibbled holes in the fabric. She got one of the other drawers open and found a pair of old boots.

Omnia swatted the dust off the chair that stood by the table and sat down.

She tried to imagine what this room would have been like without the ivy growing up against the window, when whoever had eaten that last meal had sat at this chair. Light, bright, instead of sunk in deep shadow. The window open, a parrot singing in the cage, perhaps, and the sun falling across the wood panelling on the wall behind her. Or maybe not. It must have been at night, because a pair of candles had been burning.

Was it Basilica who had sat here that night? Or was it the man whose shirts and boots still lay in the drawer? Basilica's brother? Or someone else?

Basilica knew this room, Omnia was certain of it. She knew the paintings. Basilica had been here. Perhaps she had sat in this very chair, if not on the last night, then on some other occasion.

But time had moved on since then, thought Omnia. A lot of time. It was still moving on. Second by second, minute by minute, towards the final hour. Tonight, what would happen to her?

She didn't want to go to the Silent Cloister by herself, but she couldn't take Evergrow with her. That would just put him in danger as well. This had to be done, and if it had to be done, she had to do it alone. But that didn't mean she wasn't scared. A game of deadly chess had been going on between herself and the killer, and they had reached the final stage. Each of them had one move left. Whoever miscalculated would lose.

At that very moment, she thought, Cornelius Slinker was

probably doing exactly the same thing, sitting in some hidden place, calculating, plotting what he would do that night. She remembered the shadow that had passed across the hole in the roof after the tile fell in the Hall of Leaning, the grip of his hand on her shoulder at the Slate Tower, the hiss that came from under his hood, the sound of his boots on the roof of the Ribbled Lodge. She remembered his face gazing up at her from the bottom of the Blue House as the hood fell back from his head, the height of four flights of stairs separating them. He always looked so severe, so cold. The face of a killer. Now she could almost *feel* him thinking in some darkened place, calculating, planning, just like herself.

But was he alone or was there someone else behind all of this? Pedagogia's words gnawed at her. Basilica might not have been talking nonsense, but she could still be using her? And what about the killer? Was she using him as well?

What if she was? What was the plan? How did Basilica expect to get to the Captain's treasure? And why, of all things, did she need Omnia involved?

Sometimes it was hard to believe that Basilica even existed, high up in the Slate Tower, where no one else ever came or went. But she had saved Omnia twice. But what if she had saved her only to use her? Maybe there really was no one who was trying to kill her and that was just how it was supposed to seem. Maybe the whole point was to allow Basilica to save her in order to build her trust so Basilica could use her for her own purpose. But what was it? What could Basilica possibly need her to do?

Pedagogia's words wouldn't go away, no matter how hard Omnia tried to suppress them. Omnia hadn't meant to mention Basilica to the headmistress – her name had just come out. And now Pedagogia's words kept breaking into Omnia's thoughts, and Omnia had to keep telling herself that they were wrong.

But she didn't *know* that they were wrong. The truth was, she simply didn't know. It was possible Basilica was using her in some way. And it was also possible that Basilica wasn't, and that Pedagogia had just said those things out of the hatred she obviously felt for the other woman.

There was only one thing Omnia did know. Soon it would be over, whoever was behind it, whatever the reason, whether she was being used or not. Soon the last moves in this horrible game would be made. At midnight, in only a few more hours, the game would be done. But whether she would live to tell anyone how it finished, that Omnia couldn't say.

Later, Evergrow came back with food. Omnia didn't feel much like eating. Nor did Evergrow. He said he had to go out. Something to do with a promise he had made to play a round or two of Bracketball with a few other boys. Omnia said she probably wouldn't be leaving until after eleven, so he needn't hurry if he wanted to be back before she left. Evergrow said the game might go on for hours and he might be even later than that.

They were both lying to each other.

Evergrow went, but not to play Bracketball. Omnia waited, but not until eleven.

A few minutes after Evergrow had left, she went to the window. Darkness had fallen, but the moon was yet to rise.

Now the time is fast approaching when Omnia Halibut must meet her nemesis, the person who missed her by centimetres with a tile from the roof of the Hall of Leaning, who threw her off the top of the Slate Tower, who tracked and nearly caught her in her hiding place beneath the rafters of the Ribbled Lodge. And when she meets him, she has planned that apart from the Butler and the UnderButlers who will supposedly be hiding in the Silent Cloister to witness the event, she will be alone.

Omnia hoists herself out the window, climbs down through the ivy on the wall of the Middle Range, and hurries away.

22

Night of the Black Condor

The Captain's Keep was a high, square block of a building. In the early days of the House it had been used frequently for festivities, but later Halibuts disliked it and the Keep was used now only on occasions required by ancient tradition, such as the funeral feast for the Hereditary Butler. A staircase built into the wall ran up one side of the building all the way to the roof. In the past, Omnia had climbed it on her way to the picnics the dead Butler had given for the children of the House. The reason she was climbing it now, in the darkness, was because of something she knew from having been up there before. From the roof of the Keep, you could look down over the entrances to the Silent Cloister.

The Cloister had two entrances. One was the covered walkway that ran from the Court of the Spouted Fountain. The other was a passage along the side of the Purple Nave. Unless he came out of the Great Tower itself, the only door of which opened into the Cloister, it was along one of these entrances that the killer would have to come. But Omnia wasn't going to be waiting for him there.

The strategy Omnia had decided on was that she would not enter the Silent Cloister before the killer, but after him, once she had seen him go past. Last time, at the Slate Tower, she had arrived at the time she was told, done as was expected, and almost paid the price. This time, rather than waiting for him in the Silent Cloister as he would expect, he would be the one to arrive first, and she would have the advantage of surprise on her side.

The roof of the Keep was deserted. Omnia went to the corner opposite the top of the stairs and looked down from the parapet that ran around the edge of the roof. Directly below her were trees, dark in the shadows of the moonless night. The tallest trees reached almost to the top of the building.

Looking across the House, Omnia could see lighted rooms, and here and there a glimpse of someone moving past a window. Doors opened and closed around the Great Kitchen Court, showing light for a moment, as servants went in and out. Tomorrow was Planque Day and the chefs in the kitchens would work all night in preparation. Lamps glowed in the windows of the Bright Tower where the Butlery clerks were still at their desks. Halibuts and servants were going about their business without any idea of the events unfolding at the very centre of the House.

It was nine o'clock. Three hours to go. Omnia settled down behind the parapet to wait.

After a while the moon rose, three-quarters full, sending its light over a cloudless sky. Now the scene became clearer. Directly below, running out from under the trees beside the Keep, was the covered walkway. At its end it joined the roof of the Silent Cloister, which stood like the thickly drawn border of a square at the foot of the Great Tower. Omnia could see all of it apart from one segment near the end of the covered walkway that was hidden from her view by an adjacent building. The Cloister's pool glittered in the moonlight. Above it, the Tower soared into the sky, one side lit by the moon, another side in shadow. Rooftops and courtyards surrounded it. The vaulted roof of the Purple Nave rose from their midst, and Omnia could see the first part of the passage that ran to the Cloister along the side of the Nave.

At its other end, the covered walkway started at the Court of the Spouted Fountain. The dry fountain, deep in shadow, was a dark mass. High above the court, Omnia could see the four horned shapes at the corners of the Unicorn House. They were pale in the moonlight, as if about to come alive in the darkness and leap off their plinths.

But Omnia merely glanced at them and her gaze moved on. Like a bird perched on a parapet looking for its prey, she constantly scanned the scene below her, the Cloister, the passage, the Court of the Spouted Fountain, the entrance to the covered walkway and back to the Cloister.

Now and again there was movement. Occasionally

someone went in or out of the Unicorn House. People walked across the square, by themselves or in small groups, but none entered the walkway. Omnia could see the hands on one of the clocks of the Narrow Tower. Shortly after eleven, she saw someone enter the Court, dressed in black. The figure headed straight for the covered walkway. Omnia watched. The figure was too small to be Slinker. It looked like a child. Omnia eyes went wide. *Evergrow!* What was he *doing*? Before she could do anything, he disappeared into the covered walkway.

She turned to the Cloister. A minute later, she saw him emerge, stand for a moment near the pool and then disappear under the roof.

Omnia almost groaned aloud. The best she could hope for was that Evergrow would stay hidden until everything was over. But if Cornelius Slinker was already down there, if he had seen Evergrow come in, he might decide that a trap was being set. Or worse, when midnight came, he might mistake Evergrow for her!

Omnia watched. Nothing happened at the Cloister. No one moved. There wasn't a sound.

Time passed. Omnia kept glancing back at the Cloister. She looked at the clock. Eleven thirty. She scanned the shadows below her. All was dark except for the twinkling eye of the Cloister's pool. She looked carefully along the length of the passage beside the Nave. Maybe Cornelius Slinker was watching from somewhere as well. What kind of plan would he devise? She looked along the top of the

Purple Nave. From her perch at the corner of the Captain's Keep she looked carefully across the roof of the Unicorn House. She studied the other roofs below her, searching for a movement, an irregularity, anything that would betray him.

Omnia could feel the tension in her body rising. Ten minutes to midnight. Almost time. Within the next few minutes, something would happen. It had to.

Five minutes to midnight. Surely he must be somewhere below her by now. The moonlight was strong enough for her to see him as soon as he emerged from the shadows. He might be on the segment of the Cloister's roof that was hidden from her view, but if he was there, he must have been there for hours, from before she arrived at the Keep, because otherwise she would have seen him making his way there. Omnia watched, her gaze moving slowly over the scene. Another few minutes went by. Her concentration was so intense, she didn't notice the shadow that slipped across the moonlit roofs below her. Not the first time.

But she noticed the second time

A shadow? Omnia glanced over her shoulder.

Something blotted out the moon, something dark plummeting out of the sky. Omnia jumped up. The bird, the great condor! In an instant it was on the roof behind her. But now a man stood on the roof, face hidden by a hood. Omnia's mind froze, struggling to understand. What had she actually seen in the sky – bird or man?

He took a step towards her.

242

Omnia edged back. She was hard up against the parapet. The man came a few steps closer, warily, noiselessly. He stood between her and the stairs on the other side of the roof. Not taking her eyes off him, Omnia felt behind her. She climbed on the parapet. There was nowhere further back for her to go. The man was still, his face hidden within the shadow of his hood, watching her, getting ready to move. Omnia could hear his breathing. He came a step closer. Then another step. He hissed from under his hood.

Omnia watched. The next movement would bring them together.

He lunged. Omnia tried to skip sideways and leap past him back on to the roof, but her foot slipped on the parapet and suddenly she was over the edge and falling through the tree below, gasping, grabbing for something solid as leaves and twigs slipped through her fingers, jolting and banging, and then she crashed into a series of branches and somehow she stopped, face up, back arched over a branch.

Silence.

Where was he now? Omnia looked up, trying to quell the heaviness of her breathing. Through a chink in the leaves, she could see his dark, hooded form bent over the parapet, moving right and left. He was looking for her. Carefully, Omnia turned her head and glanced towards the Cloister. She could see the roof through the branches. Below that roof, she knew, was at least one person who could help her, and hopefully more. She could call to them now. But if she called to them, the person above her would hear, and by the time they reached the Keep, he would have run down the stairs and disappeared, and the chance to unmask him would have slipped through her fingers.

Omnia glanced up again. She could see him still trying to spot her. The roof of the covered walkway ran towards the Cloister. She wasn't far above it. She measured the distance to the Cloister with her eyes. It would take time for him to climb down through the tree. By the time he did that, she might just be able to get there.

Slowly, very cautiously, Omnia raised herself on the branch. She looked back up. He must have heard her moving. He had shifted a little along the roof, trying to find her. Quietly, slowly, Omnia lowered herself until she was hanging from the branch by her hands. She glanced up again.

He was still. He knew something was happening.

Omnia took a deep breath. Then she let go of the branch, dropped, hit the walkway and ran.

Almost at once she heard him hit the roof of the walkway and she knew he was just behind her. She didn't understand how he could have got there so quickly but there was no time to think about that now. Instinctively she twisted just as she felt a hand clutching at her. She heard him stumble. She raced for her life. He was after her again. The Cloister was too far away. She wasn't going to make it.

Suddenly something reared up in front of her from around the corner of the roof at the end of the walkway. Another black figure. There were two of them! The new one ran towards her. She got ready to crash into him. He swerved and let her past. She stumbled and kept going. In another moment she was on the roof of the Cloister. She looked back. The two hooded men were grappling on the roof of the covered walkway. The first was driving the second hard towards the Cloister. The second was falling back, slipping. They were at the end of the walkway now. A blade flashed. There was a cry. A body fell from the roof into the Cloister and hit the ground.

His hood slipped back as he fell. It was Cornelius Slinker.

Omnia stared. The man still standing on the roof behind her, he was the first one. Wasn't he? The one who had hissed, who had tried to get her. She was sure he was. But it was Slinker on the ground. Which meant . . .

The man charged. Omnia ran, heading around the roof of the Cloister. A moment later, she was aware that her pursuer had stopped again. Below them, from under the roof of the Cloister, four figures had appeared. The Butler and the three UnderButlers. From behind another pillar came Evergrow.

The killer was motionless, as if wondering what to do. Omnia watched him, breathing heavily. Then he lunged for her.

Omnia jumped, leaping out as far as she could and aiming for the pool. She landed with a splash.

She came up soaked, waist-deep in water.

'That's him!' cried Omnia to the Butler. 'He killed your father.'

'Who are you?' shouted the Butler. 'Show your face!'

The man on the roof didn't respond. He looked down into the Cloister for a moment, his face still hidden by his hood, then turned his head away.

Omnia glanced in the direction in which he was gazing. It was the point where the Great Tower rose above the roof of the Cloister. There was a window in the wall of the Tower, just above the roof, the window at which the Butler had announced the death of his father.

To this day, no one knows exactly who moved first, the man on the roof or Omnia, and even if I had been there – and I'm not saying that I was, of course – I doubt I would be able to say either. Perhaps they both moved at the same instant, knowing exactly what the other was thinking. The man ran for the window above the roof of the Cloister. Omnia splashed out of the pond, soaking wet, and ran for the door beneath it.

A moment later, Digby ran after her, followed by the UnderButlers. 'Stay here!' one of them yelled at Evergrow.

Omnia heard the glass of the window above the roof smashing. She pushed on the door and an instant later was on the stairs.

She took them two at a time. Then the next flight. She caught a glimpse of the killer's cape flapping around the corner at the top of the flight as she turned the corner at the bottom. Omnia could hear him moving up the stairs ahead of her. He kept going. So did she, using all the energy that remained to her, forcing herself up. Up, up, up. Flight after flight. Her legs ached with a deep, burning pain. She knew she was slowing down, yet still she kept going. She only had to get to the top. There was no way down for the killer if he was trapped up there. He was cornered. He was finished. If only this excruciating, agonising climb would end.

The stairs got steeper. Each step was an ordeal. Finally she turned a corner and there, at the top of the steps, was a door. With a final surge of energy she ran to the door and burst through it.

The wind hit her, howling, and almost knocked her flat. The caped figure stood at one edge of the roof.

'You're cornered now,' shouted Omnia. 'Give up!'

A laugh came from beneath the man's hood. The wind flapped at his cape.

'It's over!' cried Omnia.

Digby emerged from the doorway. He stood, panting.

The wind howled across the roof of the tower. The man climbed on to the parapet at the edge of the roof.

'Don't jump!' cried Omnia.

The man spread his arms, as if to ask who would dare to come and stop him. As his arms rose, the cape billowed in the wind. Then the man leaped , but instead of falling, the wind took him up, stretching the cape under his arms and stiffening it like a pair of wings.

And Omnia knew what she was looking at. The condor, the great black bird that had been seen flying above the Tower. This was it. Not a bird, but a man.

The three UnderButlers staggered on to the roof, panting, wheezing, just in time to see him rise.

The wind took him up, and around, and into the moonlight. And then suddenly the wind gusted, and the hood blew back, and they saw his face.

It was Tobias Hildegrew.

The Butler stared in horror. Tobias threw his head back, hovering twenty metres away in the air, and fixed the Butler with a gaze full of hatred and contempt. He had nothing to lose. If the wind hadn't gusted, he might have escaped and then returned to the Butler's side undetected. But his identity had been revealed. There was no way back for him now.

He opened his mouth and shouted. His words carried to them on the wind.

'The Evergones will win. The Evergones *will win*!'

He gazed at the Butler an instant longer, then Tobias Hildegrew turned, dipped his shoulder and the wind took him away. Out of his cape fell two objects. They glittered in the moonlight as they dropped, the two keys that he had copied from the men he murdered.

The Butler slumped to his knees, face contorted in disbelief.

Omnia watched, bruised and scratched from her fall through the trees, soaking wet from her plunge into the pool, shivering in the wind as Tobias Hildegrew glided above the buildings of the House and then over the estate and out of sight. She knew that the wind would soon take him beyond the wall, beyond her reach, away from Neversuch House and all that he had done there.

'Where is he?' gasped Evergrow, running out on to the roof.

But before Omnia could say anything, the three UnderButlers surrounded her.

'You!' said Trimbleby, gazing down at her severely and poking a finger in her face. 'Not a word!'

23

Behind the UnderButlers' Door

They took her down the stairs of the Great Tower, Trimbleby in front, Dish and Withers behind. Digby stumbled down the stairs behind them in a daze at what he had seen. At the bottom, Trimbleby opened a door off the staircase and the other two UnderButlers bundled Omnia through. They let Digby in and then closed the door in the face of Evergrow, who had scrambled down the stairs after them.

Almost at once Trimbleby opened another door and a corridor stretched ahead of them. They went through more doors and each time the corridor continued. Omnia had no idea where they were going. All she knew was that they were in some kind of passage she knew nothing about, and it must run from the Great Tower through the walls of one building to the next without being visible from the outside or obvious from within. Where did it go? Eventually another door opened and she found herself in a corridor with open doors on either side through which she could see shelfloads of boxes and dusty files. Even now, in the middle of the night, clerks sat at lamplit desks and worked at the accounts of the House.

Trimbleby led the procession around one corner, and another, and finally came to a green door. He opened it and stood back as Withers and Dish pushed Omnia inside. Digby went in and then Trimbleby entered and closed the door behind him.

There were three huge desks in the room, one on each side and one facing the entrance. The desks were entirely clear and spotless. Any file that came to the UnderButlers' office – which is where Omnia had been brought – went immediately into the Butler's overflowing in-trays or to the office of the Master Filer, from where it went to the clerks' overflowing desks. The UnderButlers themselves rarely even opened them.

Trimbleby pulled a chair from beside the wall and put it in the middle of the room. 'Sit!' he said. He leaned closer. 'You heard me. *Sit!*'

Omnia sat. The three UnderButlers stood around her.

'Now tell us what you saw up there.'

Omnia told him.

All three of the UnderButlers shook their heads.

'That's what I saw!' said Omnia. 'You can ask Mr Digby.'

'What you *saw*,' said Trimbleby, without giving the

251

Butler a moment to answer, 'was Tobias Hildegrew falling from the Tower.'

'That's not what I saw.'

'Well, it's what *I* saw,' said Trimbleby.

'And me,' said Withers. 'And Mr Dish too, if I'm not mistaken.'

Dish nodded.

'But I saw him—'

'Falling from the Tower,' said Trimbleby. 'Understand? Nothing else.'

Omnia didn't understand. She glanced at the Butler again. He avoided her eyes.

'Hildegrew's gone,' said Withers. 'It's just the same as if he's dead. What's the point in alarming the House?'

'What if he comes back?'

'How can he? Everyone here knows him. He could never show his face.'

Omnia stared at the UnderButlers in amazement. 'Aren't you going after him?'

'And do what?' demanded Trimbleby sarcastically. 'Chase him? By now he'll be in the city. There are a thousand places he could go.'

'Then go there as well!'

The three UnderButlers looked at each other and laughed.

'What?' demanded Omnia.

'We're not the authority in the city, Omnia Halibut,' said Trimbleby. 'Our authority ends at the wall. Out there, we can't just search wherever we want.'

'Besides,' said Withers, 'he'll keep going. They always do. Soon he'll be on a boat. Next week he'll be a thousand miles away. Gone forever. That's good enough for us. What more can we ask for?'

'But he wasn't doing this alone!' said Omnia incredulously. 'It wasn't just him. He was the bird.'

'Yes, that's obvious now, isn't it? We don't need you to tell us that.'

'Well, where was he going every time?' demanded Omnia. It wasn't just once that the so-called black condor had been seen to fly on the wind. Each time Hildegrew had flown, Omnia realised, he had been secretly leaving the House. It all made sense now. He left on the wind that blew at the top of the Great Tower, and when he came back, he crept in through the wall behind the South Wood. He was the figure she had glimpsed on the morning after Everwise's funeral, not Cornelius Slinker. He was the one who had used the gap in the wall.

But if Tobias Hildegrew was going in and out secretly, surely it was with a purpose. There must have been a reason he had to leave the House.

'What if he was meeting someone outside?' demanded Omnia. 'Someone who knew what was going on? Someone who was telling him what to do?' That was what Basilica had suggested, and what other explanation could there be for the way he had come and gone?

'What if he was?'

'Well . . .' Omnia was almost speechless with disbelief. 'How can you just forget about it?'

253

The UnderButlers didn't reply.

'Who are the Evergones?' she demanded. 'Tobias Hildegrew said they'd win.'

'He did not!'

'He did!' retorted Omnia incredulously. First they denied what she knew she had seen, now what she had heard. 'I heard him. Who are they?'

Trimbleby glanced at the other UnderButlers.

'How old is she?' asked Trimbleby quietly.

'I'm twelve and a quarter,' said Omnia.

The UnderButlers ignored her. Dish went to a cupboard and pulled out a ledger and began to flick quickly through the pages.

'I'm twelve and a quarter!'

Dish came to a stop and ran his finger down a page. 'She's twelve and a quarter.'

Withers took a deep breath and shook his head gravely. 'Young. *Much* too young.'

Trimbleby nodded. 'Even as an exception.'

'Too young for what?' demanded Omnia. She glanced at Digby when she saw the UnderButler weren't going to tell her. 'Too young for what?'

The Butler didn't reply. He was sitting on the edge of one of the desks, staring at the floor, eyes vacant, as if reliving those last minutes at the top of the Tower, the wind blowing the hood away from Tobias Hildegrew's face, the look of scorn that Hildegrew had given him, the sense of almost inconceivable betrayal that he felt.

'Listen to me,' said Trimbleby.

Omnia looked back with a start.

'There are things you're too young to know. But understand this. He's not the first. There's not just one. There's many. This is how we can stop them.'

'You mean the Evergones, don't you?'

'I'm not saying what I mean.'

'Well, I know! It wasn't just him. Basilica Halibut told me.'

'Basilica who?' said Withers.

'Basilica Halibut!'

Withers laughed. 'There's no such person. There was, many years ago. But she died. Eighteen years ago or thereabouts. An accident wasn't it, Mr Dish?'

Dish nodded, stroking his cheeks. 'Freakish.'

'That's not true! She's alive. I saw her in the Slate Tower only two days ago.'

'No one lives in the Slate Tower.'

'Basilica Halibut does.'

'No, that's where she died.'

Omnia stared.

'And that servant of hers as well. What was his name again?' Withers clicked his fingers. 'Winifred? Winigrew?'

'Winnicott,' said Dish.

'That's it. Winnicott. They died together. I can remember the day. Terrible accident. Something to do with a fishing net, wasn't it?' Withers looked back at Omnia. 'You must have seen their ghosts. You know what they say. Ghosts haunt the places where they died.'

'She wasn't a ghost,' said Omnia.

'She didn't give you any food, did she?'

'What if she did?'

'You know what they say. Ghosts always use food to tempt people. Eat it and you'll turn into a ghost yourself.'

Omnia was silent, remembering the table laden with strange, delicious breakfast foods. And she had eaten a slice of exactly the same pie that Basilica had eaten.

'Perhaps you'd like to tell us how you found her,' said Trimbleby.

'I fell off the Tower and . . .' Omnia stopped.

'How?'

Omnia didn't reply.

'Perhaps you'd like to show us.'

Omnia shook her head.

'What's that?' demanded Trimbleby.

'No,' she whispered.

'No what?'

'No, I don't want to show you how I found her.'

'Sure?'

She nodded. For the second time in twenty-four hours, she had blurted out Basilica's name. First Pedagogia, now the UnderButlers. It would be the worst thing she could do, Basilica had said, for both of them.

Trimbleby watched her to see if she was going to say anything else. 'Now Tobias Hildegrew is dead as well. Understand? Fell from the top of the Great Tower. Done. Finished. That's all anybody needs to know. Hildegrew's gone. We stopped them this time like we've stopped them before. That's enough. We can't do any more.'

But it wasn't enough. Omnia turned to the Butler. 'He killed your father!'

'Did he?' said Trimbleby. 'Where's the proof?'

'You know he did,' said Omnia, still staring at the Butler.

'No,' said Withers. 'Old Mr Digby fell, he rolled, he drowned.'

'An accident,' said Dish. 'Freakish.'

'And what about Cornelius Slinker?' demanded Omnia, suddenly remembering what she had seen on the roof of the covered walkway. 'You *saw* what Tobias did to him!'

'Did we?' retorted Trimbleby. 'I saw Cornelius fall off a roof. At midnight. What was he doing there in the first place, I'd like to know?'

'A man who creeps around on roofs at midnight is almost bound to come to a violent end,' said Withers.

'Almost bound to,' said Dish.

'He was protecting *me*!' cried Omnia. All at once she realised it. Omnia hadn't had a moment to think about it until now, but it was clear what he had been doing. He had grappled with Hildegrew, and if not for him, it would have been her body that had been flung from the roof.

'If we go after Hildegrew,' said Withers, 'if we go out there and make accusations about a murder in the House, the authorities in the city will demand to come in. That's all they're waiting for. They've been waiting for years. All they need—'

'That's enough, Mr Withers!' snapped Trimbleby. 'That's quite enough. She doesn't need to know any of that.' He turned to Omnia. 'You, you're a Halibut. You leave this to us.'

'What's *that* supposed to mean?' shouted Omnia, and she sprang up from the chair. Trimbleby pushed her back. Omnia struggled, but Trimbleby held her down. Yet he wasn't even looking at her now, keeping her in her seat with a single heavy hand. He and the other two UnderButlers had turned to Digby, and seemed to have lost interest in her. They were saying something. Omnia stopped shouting and listened to what was being said.

'The House goes on, Mr Digby,' said Withers.

The Butler gazed blankly at the three UnderButlers.

'You know it does. Despite everything. This isn't the first time something like this has happened. Far from it. Your father knew the risks. The House goes on, that's what he would have said. Like his father, and his father, all the way back to your great-great-great-great-great-great-great-grandfather.'

'It's true, Mr Digby,' said Dish. 'The House goes on.'

There was silence. Then Digby nodded. 'The House goes on,' he said quietly, as Hereditary Butlers had said for centuries before him.

'Now perhaps you'll trust us,' said Trimbleby, 'like your father did.'

'That's all we've been asking you to do all along,' said Withers.

'Nothing more,' added Dish.

Digby nodded again.

Omnia watched for a moment longer. Then she yelled. 'Get your hand *off* me!'

Trimbleby turned back to Omnia as if he had forgotten all about her. 'Are you going to scream? Are you going to kick?'

Omnia gazed at him with angry, narrowed eyes.

'All right.' Trimbleby took his hand away. 'Now, there was a report you were seen outside the wall. I take it that was false. I take it that was a rumour Hildegrew started.'

Omnia nodded, rubbing at her shoulder.

'Where were you hiding?'

Omnia didn't reply.

'Well, there are plenty of places, aren't there? So, about this rumour, we'll say it was a mistake, shall we?'

'A mistake,' said Withers. 'No one should have any suspicions about you.'

'How does that sound?' said Dish.

Omnia shrugged.

'You could show a bit more gratitude,' remarked Trimbleby.

'Thank you,' muttered Omnia, barely able to bring herself to utter the words.

'And what does Evergrow know? He came to us and said you knew who killed the Butler.'

'He thinks it was Cornelius Slinker.'

'What about Basilica? Did Evergrow see— I mean, did he see her ghost as well?'

Omnia shook her head.

The UnderButlers watched her closely.

'It was me by myself!'

The UnderButlers watched her for a moment longer, then they huddled together. Omnia strained to hear what they said.

'The boy didn't see Tobias go,' whispered Withers.

'He was too late for that,' added Dish.

Trimbleby nodded. 'He'll believe Tobias fell as long as *she* doesn't tell him.'

'What if he goes around saying the Butler was murdered?' said Dish.

'Where's the proof?' said Withers.

'And who will he say it to?' Trimbleby laughed. 'The Halibuts?'

The others grinned.

Suddenly Trimbleby turned back to her. 'Tell us again what you saw tonight at the Great Tower.'

'I saw Tobias Hildegrew fly away.'

Trimbleby took a deep breath, struggling to control himself.

'It would be a terrible thing if it turned out the rumour about you being outside the wall was true,' said Withers. 'Do you know what the punishment would be?'

'You can't punish a Halibut!' cried Omnia.

'Can we *not*?' demanded Trimbleby scornfully. 'Have we not done it before? The punishment for someone who goes outside the wall never ends, Omnia Halibut. It lasts your whole life.'

'Don't you know what it is?' said Withers. 'You're a clever girl. What would someone like that deserve? Can't you work it out?'

Dish watched her, one eyebrow raised on his basset-like face.

The Butler came forward. 'Omnia,' he said. 'Be sensible. Tell us what you saw.'

'I saw Tobias Hildegrew . . .'

'You saw him fall from the Tower,' said Digby. 'Isn't that right?'

Omnia was silent.

'Say it!' said Trimbleby.

'Mr Trimbleby, that's enough,' said Digby. He came closer to her. 'Omnia, there are reasons . . . Some things are bigger than either of us. The House goes on.' He crouched in front of her in his long green coat. 'Omnia, you saw him fall. If I can say that, after everything that's happened, after my own father's death at the hands of this man, surely you can.'

Omnia frowned.

'Omnia? Please.' The Butler gave her a helpless smile. 'I'm asking you to understand. There are things we need to do sometimes, that we don't want to do, but we need to do them. Not for you or for me, but for everyone. I don't necessarily want to be the Butler, but here I am. I have to do it. For the House.' He paused. 'Please, Omnia.'

Omnia looked at the Butler. His eyes pleaded with her.

261

'You saw him fall, didn't you? Omnia? Didn't you?'

Omnia took a deep breath. She nodded. 'I saw him fall.'

'Louder!' demanded Trimbleby.

The Butler stood up. 'That's enough, Mr Trimbleby.' He glanced at Omnia. 'I trust her. She knows what she has to say. Now, Mr Dish, perhaps you can show Omnia out.'

Dish looked at the other two UnderButlers.

'Mr Dish?'

Dish nodded.

Omnia got up.

'You say anything wrong – I'll know about it,' growled Trimbleby as Omnia went to the door. 'I'll be watching you all the time.'

Dish led her along a corridor, around one corner, another corner, then down another corridor lined with offices and around more corners and down more corridors until finally they reached the room with the clock where Evergrow had waited two days before. The two Clerks of the Entrance got up sleepily from behind the desk and hastily smoothed the rumples in their walnut-coloured coats. The junior clerk, who was dozing on his chair, looked around with a start.

'For your own good, Omnia, remember what we said.' Dish looked down at her seriously. His drooping jowls made him look like a very stern basset hound. 'It's not a joke. You won't get any second chances.' He paused and then pointed at the door. 'You can go. Those are the stairs.'

She went down. Outside, Omnia looked up and saw the shadow of the Bright Tower rising in the moonlight above her.

Only now did she know where she had been.

Someone was waiting for her in the doorway of the Long South Range.

'I didn't know where you'd got to so I waited here,' said Evergrow. 'Are you all right?'

Omnia nodded. She sat down on the doorstep. 'You shouldn't have been there tonight, Evergrow. I told you not to come.'

Evergrow sat beside her. 'I couldn't let you do it by yourself.'

'Well, you shouldn't have done it.'

'I'm sorry, Omnia, but I just couldn't let you go alone. Not without at least trying to help. I couldn't bear to think of you being there by yourself with that killer and no one to help you.'

'Digby and the UnderButlers were there. That was the plan, remember?'

'What if they hadn't turned up? Omnia, I know you must be angry at me, but I just couldn't—'

'Thank you, Evergrow.'

Evergrow stopped in surprise.

'That was brave of you.'

Evergrow looked at her suspiciously, wondering if she was making fun of him.

But she wasn't. Evergrow had shown courage, not just tonight, but at the Slate Tower as well. Omnia was beginning to wonder whether she had underestimated him. She had always known that he was trustworthy, but she had never thought he could be so brave.

'You're serious, aren't you?' he said.

'Everlook would be proud of you.'

Evergrow smiled at the mention of their uncle. For him there was no higher compliment. 'Do you think so?'

Omnia nodded. 'But you could have ruined everything! Don't do something like that again without telling me.'

'Don't stop me helping you again and I won't.'

Omnia watched him for a moment and then smiled. 'Fair enough.' She put out her hand.

Evergrow grinned. They shook.

'So what happened?' he said.

Omnia sighed. 'The UnderButlers just wanted to ask me a few questions.'

'No, at the top of the Tower. Who was it? Did you see?'

'Tobias Hildegrew.'

Evergrow stared in amazement. 'Tobias Hildegrew? Did he fall? Have they found his body?'

Omnia shrugged.

'But how did it happen?'

'It's hard to describe.'

'Did you fight him? Did he—'

'No. He jumped by himself.'

'He must have known he had no choice.'

264

'I suppose so. Evergrow, I'm tired. And I'm wet.' Suddenly Omnia realised that her clothes were still damp from her leap into the pond of the Silent Cloister. Besides, she didn't know what to say. She didn't want to lie. Not to Evergrow, of all people. Not after everything he had done for her.

Evergrow nodded quickly. 'Of course.' He peered at her face. 'You've got scratches.'

Omnia was silent for a moment. 'Evergrow, what did Cornelius Slinker say when you saw him yesterday? Tell me again. What did you say he said?'

'That he wanted to protect you.'

'Why?'

'He didn't say.'

'How did he know I needed help?'

Evergrow shrugged. 'Was that him tonight, the one who fell off the roof in the Cloister?'

'I think so. Did you see him when you came down?'

Evergrow shook his head. 'Someone must have already taken his body away.'

Omnia was silent again. She thought about poor Cornelius. She remembered the flash of the blade and his cry just before he fell. He had died to save her and she had never even had a chance to thank him.

She got up wearily. 'I'll see you tomorrow.'

Evergrow got up as well. 'But it really was Tobias Hildegrew who fell from the Tower? You're sure it was him?'

'It was Tobias Hildegrew.'

'And he was the one who was after you?'

'I suppose so.'

'And he killed the Captain and Digby too?'

'I don't know, Evergrow. I don't know if anyone will ever know.'

'And now he's dead?'

Omnia frowned. She had already come close to lying. She knew that she was allowing Evergrow to think something that she herself knew to be untrue, and if that wasn't a lie in itself, it was almost as bad. She didn't want to make it worse.

'I'm tired,' she said. 'I'm really tired, Evergrow.'

Evergrow nodded. 'Well, if he's dead, you won't need to hide any more, anyway.'

'Hopefully not.'

'It was fun in a way, don't you think?'

Omnia looked at him doubtfully.

'You having to hide . . . me bringing you food . . .'

'Let's try it the other way round next time.'

Evergrow grinned. 'If you ever need somewhere to hide again, my wardrobe's always free.'

Omnia smiled as well. 'Thanks, Evergrow. I mean for everything. And by the way, don't tell anyone you ever saw Basilica. Especially the UnderButlers, if they ask you. I told them you never met her.'

Evergrow looked at her quizzically.

'I'm going to bed. I'll see you tomorrow.'

'It's Planque Day. Are you going to come?'

'I'll see.'

Omnia went inside. She climbed the stairs and went down the corridor to her family's apartment. She crept past the closed door of the room where her parents were sleeping, then past her brother's room. To judge by the aroma wafting from under Eversmooth's door, he was hard at work experimenting with some new oleaginous concoction. Omnia reached her own room and finally, for what seemed like the first time in weeks, lay down in a real bed.

And extraordinarily enough, after all that had happened, Omnia soon fell into a deep, dreamless sleep – whether through sheer exhaustion or because there was so much to think about that her mind simply gave up trying to understand it, I really couldn't say.

24

Above the Planque

The day was sunny and warm, as the day of Everwise's funeral had been just over a week previously. The wind that had sprung up overnight, and which had howled with such fury at the top of the Great Tower, had died down, leaving only a gentle, teasing breeze.

All over the vast roof of the Burdock House sat Haliburts. It was Planque Day, named in honour of a game invented by Everdew Halibut the Second, which involved one team throwing quoits at reindeer antlers worn by the opposing team. The game was played on the cobbles of the court in the centre of the Burdock House, and traditionally the spectators sat on the roof overlooking the court, legs hanging over the edge, beating their feet whenever they wanted to applaud on a wooden ledge that had been attached to the wall below them specifically for the purpose. Planque wasn't played by the young, but by the old. Every year, a number of teams consisting of the older Halibuts competed, the most ancient of whom were scarcely able to walk and sat in various places around the court, feebly waving their heads to avoid the quoits being tossed at the antlers they wore by throwers who were equally unable to move from the spots where they had been positioned. None of the Halibut children had any interest in the game, and it was rare indeed for anyone to show the slightest enthusiasm for it before the age of forty or to take it up before they were sixty.

Yet almost every Halibut came, if not to compete, and if not to watch the tournament, then to enjoy the Planque Feast, which was served on the roof after the last of the games was over. Even now, as the games were in progress, Digby and the UnderButlers were overseeing the laying of rows of tables that stood on the roof behind the backs of the Halibuts watching the game in the courtyard below. Servers in scarlet tunics swarmed around the tables with crockery, cutlery and platters of food. More servers stood at a corner of the roof where a winch had been set up to raise the makings of the feast from the ground. The food was brought to the foot of the building by a steady stream of cooks who came and went from the kitchen like a line of white ants coming and going from their nest.

In the days of Everdew Halibut the Second, the games went on all day and the feast was a simple meal that lasted an hour. Nowadays, the games were over by noon, and the feasting was a prolonged gluttony that lasted into the night.

Omnia stood with a number of the other children and

gazed into the courtyard over the heads of enthusiastic Halibut adults who were stamping their feet on the boards. A quoit snagged on an antler and they stamped in approval. Omnia looked up. She saw Digby and the Prime Server standing at one of the tables, conferring about something. The three UnderButlers stood in various places around the roof. Each of them threw a watchful glance in her direction.

'This is so boring!' said Eversmart, who was wearing a shirt with exceptionally wide orange stripes, and he looked longingly at the tables behind them, wondering how much longer it was going to be before they could start eating.

'I don't call this a sport,' said Artesia, who was equally bored.

'I do,' said Evesia.

'Who cares what any of you think?' snapped Eversniff Halibut, the grumpiest man in the House, who was among the group sitting in front of them. 'You'll appreciate it when you grow up.'

'I'd rather not grow up if it means I'm going to appreciate it,' muttered Eversmart.

Eversniff turned around and glared.

Eversmart was right, thought Omnia. Imagine growing up to like Planque. Imagine growing up to actually want to play it.

Omnia walked away across the roof. She stopped and gazed at the Great Tower. It was such a pleasant day. There was no hint of what had happened up there the previous night. Standing in the sunshine, with the breeze gently

270

caressing her face, it was hard to believe that scene wasn't something she had imagined, the darkness, the howling wind, the birdlike shape jumping from the roof.

Yet it had happened, and it wasn't her imagination. And what had happened afterwards wasn't her imagination either. Although it would be easy, thought Omnia, very easy, to begin to believe that it was. Less than twenty-four hours had passed and already rumours were spreading, already things were being said in the House that made her doubt what she knew to be true. She almost thought she would have to write the whole thing down if she wanted to remember what had really happened.

In the morning, by the time she woke up, the rumour was already spreading that she had never been outside the wall. The allegation was now known to have been the result of a mistaken identity. When she saw her parents for the first time in days, they couldn't remember exactly when they had last seen her, and when she said she had gone to stay with Evergrow for a few days, they seemed perfectly satisfied with the explanation. They were more interested in another rumour that was going around.

Apparently, Tobias Hildegrew had fallen to his death from the top of the Great Tower during the night and had been hastily buried, so mangled was his body. There was a fresh grave in the Meadow of Rest to prove it. People were saying that he had gone up the Tower to try to catch the black condor, not giving a thought to his own safety, so selfless and loyal a servant had he been. Evertwitch

271

N Halibut opined that the condor could certainly have lifted him with its claws, so gigantic a bird was it, and that probably he had fallen from its grip in a titanic struggle above the House. Evermay vowed to paint a magnificent picture of his heroic death to commemorate him forever as one of the House's most outstanding serv-ants. Everyone would miss Tobias, and there was great sadness among the Halibuts at the news of his mangled end – but not enough sadness to dampen their enjoyment of Planque Day which, after all, came but once a year. Tobias would have wanted them to enjoy it, they told each other seriously.

Omnia looked at them now, clustered around the roof of the Burdock House, and it seemed to her that she saw them as she had never seen them before. Everdean, who was the closest thing they had to a Captain, sat on the opposite edge of the roof in his blue coat, chin sunk on his chest, a young UnderUnderButler holding him up on either side so he wouldn't slump forward and fall. All around him sat other Halibuts. Omnia's own parents weren't far away, with Evergrow's parents and a group of their friends. They roared and stamped their feet in delight at something that happened on the court below. A quoit on an antler, probably. Behind them, the servants swarmed around the tables, preparing the feast.

Suddenly a thought came into Omnia's mind. *How long can this go on?*

The thought shocked her. It had never occurred to

Omnia that anything might ever change. The House had always been here, and it always would be. She was a Halibut, and this was where a Halibut lived. And this was how a Halibut lived. And so they all sat up here on Planque Day and stamped their feet and waited for the feast to begin, as it had begun every year since the time of Everdew Halibut the Second.

And yet Tobias Hildegrew had come *this* close to gaining access to the Halibut treasure. If he had got in there and taken it, what would have been left of this life they led, of the House, of everything in it? No one who was sitting up here and watching the Planque had any idea how close he had come to achieving his aim or the crimes he had committed along the way. It had been kept from them, as if they were small children – all the Halibuts, young and old – and couldn't be trusted to know the truth.

And why shouldn't a servant want the treasure? Of course. Why not?

'Omnia?'

Omnia looked around. She stared. Cornelius Slinker!

'I thought you were . . .'

Cornelius shook his head. 'Knocked me out. The fall. All right now. Nothing broken. Bit of a headache, that's all.'

'But your face . . .'

A long wound ran across Slinker's face, from the corner of his left eye all the way down to his chin. It had been

273

stitched and tiny knots studded his skin at regular intervals.

'He had a knife. Lucky. Another centimetre and he would have had my eye.'

Omnia nodded. She didn't know exactly what to say. How to start. 'I thought you were . . .'

'I know.'

'But you weren't.'

'No.'

'Why did you chase me to the Slate Tower?'

'To protect you.'

'How did you find me that morning?'

'Thought you must be with Evergrow. Waited outside the Range.'

'All night?'

Slinker nodded.

'How did you know I needed protection?'

'The tile.'

'You knew it wasn't an accident?'

'Suspected. Gondolier couldn't find a reason.' Cornelius shrugged. 'No reason for a tile to fall – tile won't fall. Someone must have helped it.'

'Why didn't anyone else think like that?'

The messenger shrugged again. 'Didn't want to?'

'And that's how you guessed that something was wrong? That's all?'

'After the rumour about you going outside the wall, I was certain. Heard the rumour – knew someone must be desperate to get you.'

'And after that you tried to protect me?'

He nodded.

'Cornelius, why didn't you tell me?'

'Told Evergrow.'

'But why didn't you tell *me*?'

'When?'

'When you were chasing me to the top of the Slate Tower!'

'Couldn't catch you.'

Omnia smiled. She almost wanted to laugh.

The messenger looked at her sheepishly. Suddenly Omnia understood that Cornelius Slinker was shy, and that was why he barely ever said a word. Not stern, not severe, just shy. And yet he had been watching over her – or trying to – ever since he realised she was in danger.

'You saved my life last night,' she said quietly.

Cornelius looked down, shifting his feet in embarrassment.

'And you almost got killed.'

Cornelius shrugged.

'Thank you.'

'No need to thank me,' he murmured, still staring downward.

'I *do* need to thank you.' Omnia said it again. 'Thank you, Cornelius. Thank you for trying to protect me. Thank you for saving my life.'

He looked up. 'You can rely on me,' he said seriously. 'Understand that, Omnia Halibut. You can rely on Cornelius Slinker. Always. Until the end.'

Omnia opened her mouth to reply.

'Cornelius Slinker!' said Evergrow, who had come over to join them. 'I thought you were dead.'

Slinker turned around. 'Just a rumour,' he murmured. 'Much exaggerated.'

'I wondered where you were when I came down from the Tower. I thought someone must have taken your body away.'

'Got up and walked,' said Slinker. 'Not too hard. Bit groggy. Fell over a couple of times. Perfectly all right now.'

'What a scar! Does it hurt?'

Slinker shook his head.

'Omnia,' said Evergrow, 'have you heard what they're saying about Tobias Hildegrew? I don't understand. Everyone's saying he was such a good man, it's such a shame he's dead, what a hero he was, how he died trying to catch the great condor. When I tell people they're wrong, they just laugh at me. But none of it's true! He killed the Butler.'

'I suppose there's no proof,' said Omnia.

'So does that mean he didn't? And does that mean he was never really after you? He came to get you last night. And he tried to kill you at the Slate Tower. Maybe the tile in the Hall of Leaning was an accident, but not what you told me about the Slate Tower. That was true, wasn't it?'

Omnia nodded.

'Then I don't understand! If he's dead, all right, at least he's gone. But why not tell the truth about him? Why make him seem so wonderful?' Evergrow looked at Cornelius. 'I'm right, aren't I? Don't you think so?'

The messenger didn't speak. Omnia watched him. He had realised she needed protection. He wasn't convinced by freakish accidents. Did that mean he had seen 'accidents' like that before? Had he seen other people chased, and caught, and killed? Perhaps, as a messenger, he had seen or heard about other things that had been hidden from the Halibuts, just as this was being concealed.

'Did he jump?' said Evergrow. 'Did he fall? Did someone push him? You, Omnia? Were you fighting with him? Did you push him over the edge?'

'I didn't push him over.'

'Did someone else? The UnderButlers?'

'No.'

'Then how did it happen?'

Omnia hesitated. Maybe she would tell, after all. She glanced at Trimbleby, who was watching her from one corner of the roof. Maybe she just would!

'It's all right,' said Evergrow, just as she was about to speak. 'I know. I shouldn't keep asking. It's upsetting. It must have been horrible to see.'

Omnia was silent. Then she nodded. She could see the corner of an envelope sticking out of the pocket of Cornelius Slinker's cloak. 'Is that his death certificate?' she asked.

Cornelius nodded.

'And you'll take it now?'

The messenger nodded again.

He would go past the West Range, Omnia thought, and then he would trot three miles until he reached the gate and then he would step out into the city beyond to take the certificate to wherever it had to go. A false death certificate, because Tobias Hildegrew wasn't dead. And what else was out there? They were. Now just one, but many. Isn't that what the Trimbleby had said? Not one, but many.

She knew who Trimbleby was talking about. The same people Basilica had been talking about, the ones Tobias Hildegrew must have been going to see whenever he flew out of the House. The Evergones. But who were they? And why did Hildegrew say they were going to win, as if they were fighting some kind of war against the House and this had been only one small battle?

Had Basilica once been one of them? When Omnia had told Pedagogia that Basilica was alive, the headmistress's first reaction was that Omnia must have seen her outside the wall. Maybe Basilica had been one of them and that was why she had been locked away. But if that was the case, Omnia felt certain that she wasn't on their side any more.

Basilica existed. That was one thing Omnia knew. She didn't care what the UnderButlers said. Basilica wasn't a ghost. Nor was she something that Omnia had simply imagined. She was unlike any other Halibut Omnia had ever met, so much so that Omnia almost wondered whether she was a Halibut at all. But she was real.

Omnia gazed at the Slate Tower, far off in the distance. She wondered whether Basilica was looking out her window now towards the Burdock House, just as she, Omnia, was looking at the windows of the Slate Tower.

It seemed to Omnia that nothing she thought she had known about the House could be trusted. Things weren't as they seemed, as Basilica had said. But Omnia realised that she didn't know which things these were, at least not all of them, and even the things she knew about she probably didn't really understand. Not yet.

She almost wished she didn't know any of it. She almost wished she could be like all the others sitting above the Planque, the Halibuts shouting in delight and stamping their feet if they were old, or muttering about their how boring it was, if they were young. All waiting for the feast, not giving a thought to anything else – as she had been until the morning barely more than a week before when she saw the hooded figure of Tobias Hildegrew coming out of the Mottled Wood, until the moment when she had decided that she had to go and investigate. That decision, she knew, had changed her life in a way that could never be changed back. And Omnia wondered now, if she had known how her life would change, would she still have decided to do it?

But what she knew now couldn't be unknown. Omnia was beginning to understand just how much had changed within her. Only three days ago, she had looked at the massive rafters of the Ribbled Lodge and reassured herself with the thought that they had been there for two hundred years, and they would be there for two hundred years more, and another two hundred years after that. And now she looked at the feast being laid behind the Halibuts on the roof of the Burdock House and found herself asking how much longer it could go on, if it all might end tomorrow.

'Well, it's over now, anyway,' said Evergrow, still thinking about Tobias Hildegrew.

Omnia looked back at him. Cornelius Slinker stood by Evergrow's side, watching her. Omnia was glad Cornelius was there. She had a feeling she would need his help again. And Evergrow's. She had a feeling she would need them both.

Omnia Halibut doesn't believe in destiny. Remember? We heard her say that when all of this was just starting, when Allevia asked her whether the name makes the person or the person makes the name. Omnia believes that a person makes her own choices. Or at least that is what she always has believed. And yet now she wonders whether there is some kind of force – call it destiny, or luck, or anything you like – that has thrown her into the heart of a struggle for the House itself, a struggle that has gone on, hidden from view, for generation after generation, and if she chooses not to play her part – if she is the one who refuses the call in her generation– then the struggle will be lost. But if she does choose to play her part, she wonders what she will lose of herself and of the life she always thought she would have.

Of course, it's hard to know exactly what a person is

thinking unless they tell you themselves. And I'm not saying Omnia ever did tell me, or that I was ever there to hear her even if she had wanted to. How I came to know about all of this is of little importance compared with the extraordinary events that befell Omnia herself, and if I do ever choose to tell that story, I'll certainly wait until I've finished this one first. Which is only fair to Omnia, as well as to everyone who has read this book.

But I do know one thing that she's thinking as she stands on the roof of the Burdock House with Evergrow and Cornelius, surrounded by Halibuts cheering and stamping at the Planque below. It isn't over. Evergrow is wrong. He didn't hear the words Tobias Hildegrew shouted at the top of the Great Tower before he turned and flew away. But Omnia did.

If anything, thinks Omnia, it's only beginning.